James Lowry Whittle

Grover Cleveland

James Lowry Whittle

Grover Cleveland

ISBN/EAN: 9783337418748

Printed in Europe, USA, Canada, Australia, Japan

Cover: Foto ©Andreas Hilbeck / pixelio.de

More available books at **www.hansebooks.com**

GROVER

CLEVELAND

PUBLIC MEN OF TO-DAY

An International Series

Edited

By

S. H. JEYES

GROVER
CLEVELAND

By

JAMES LOWRY WHITTLE

WITH TWO PORTRAITS

NEW YORK

FREDERICK WARNE & CO.

3, COOPER UNION

PREFACE

THE object of this series is to present, in a brief space, a picture of the public life of the different nations who contribute to the history of our time. This end, it is believed, may be best attained by a study of the career of some conspicuous personage in each nationality. In the case of the United States of America, there is no one now alive who has played so important a part, and who, at the same time, possesses so distinct a personality, as Grover Cleveland. He has been for many years the leader of a great political party, which returned to power after a proscription of nearly a generation. He has had the distinction—rare in modern times—of being elected twice to the highest office recognized by the Constitution.

In the earlier period of the nation's history, the election of a President for a second term was the rule. John Adams and his son were the only Presidents among the first seven who were not re-elected at the end of the four years' period;

but, of the citizens so honoured, two were soldiers,
Washington and Jackson ; whilst the other three,
Jefferson, Madison, and Monroe — "the Virginia
dynasty," as they are called by American writers
—had all taken a more or less important part in
the founding of the Republic. Since the second
election of General Jackson in 1833, there was
no instance of a second term until the Civil War,
when Lincoln was re-elected in 1864; and General
Grant, the most conspicuous soldier of the North,
received the same tribute in 1873.

Mr. Cleveland's re-election in 1892 was the first
instance in which this distinction was bestowed
upon a citizen who had no claim to military glory,
or had had no opportunity of leading in a great
political crisis, such as the Revolution or the Civil
War. The honour was the more signal from the
fact that it was not, as in the case of the seven
other Presidents who had been twice chosen to this
post, a continuation of a period of office.

For three generations the position of President
had been regarded as the culmination of a political
career. Mr. Cleveland, however, during the administration of his successor, General Harrison,
continued to be an influential figure in public life ;
and after the brief triumph of the Republican party,
he returned to the Executive Mansion, which he
had quitted in March, 1889.

The unique position he thus attained is due not

only to great personal abilities, but to the absolute confidence of his fellow-citizens in his rectitude and his independence. They believed that he would know what was right, and was certain to do it.

The Democratic Convention held at Chicago this month marks a crisis in the long battle which the President has waged for the revival of Democratic principles. For the time the party has abandoned his teaching, and adopted new leaders. This incident only brings the policy he has struggled for into stronger contrast with the cheerful self-confidence of the American man of the world. It was a favourite notion among sanguine Americans of both parties that politics did not very much matter to anybody. If things were likely to go wrong, the men of sense and position would step in, and the party managers would set everything right. But at Chicago the professional politician has himself taken the leadership of the crowd, and pays no heed to his former patrons.

Mr. Cleveland, on the other hand, always insisted that the political training of the people was a question of supreme import ; that they themselves should be addressed, and not the organizers. Infinite pains should be taken to lay the facts before them. This he maintained by precept and example, and this policy has twice made him President of the United States. It was the theory of Jefferson and Jackson, and is deeply imbedded in the life of the Republic. With the reaction against the recent mutiny will probably come a large increase of Mr. Cleveland's reputation and influence.

From the luminous essays published in the *Quarterly Journal of Political Science* I have derived great assistance, as well as from the masterly works of Professor Taussig on Tariff and Silver, and from the *Congressional Currency* of Mr. Gordon.

For the personal details of Mr. Cleveland's history, I am indebted to some hints from American friends, and to the series of popular biographies written from time to time, with his authority, by Mr. Pendleton King, Mr. Hensel, of Pennsylvania, and Mr. George F. Parker.

In conclusion, I wish to express my thanks to Mr. James Bonar, who has been good enough to read over in proof the chapters on the tariff and on currency; and to Mr. B. L. Mosely, of 2, Brick Court, Temple, who has given me valuable help in the chapters on the foreign policy of the United States.

31st July, 1896.

CONTENTS

———

CHAPTER I.

ANCESTRY AND EARLY LIFE.

CHAPTER II.

MAYORALTY OF BUFFALO.

CHAPTER III.

GOVERNORSHIP OF NEW YORK.

CHAPTER IX.

MR. CLEVELAND IN OPPOSITION.

CHAPTER X.

ELECTION FOR A SECOND TERM.

CHAPTER XI.

CURRENCY LEGISLATION.

CHAPTER XII.

OBSTRUCTION IN THE SENATE.

CHAPTER XIII.

FOREIGN RELATIONS OF THE UNITED STATES.

CHAPTER XIV.

AMERICA AND GREAT BRITAIN.

CHAPTER XV.

THE CHICAGO REVOLT.

CHRONOLOGICAL TABLE

———◆———

1837 March 18th. Grover Cleveland born at Caldwell, New Jersey.

1841 Cleveland family settle in Western New York.

1845 Death of General Jackson.

1851 Grover Cleveland employed at Fayetteville.

1853 Oct. 1st. Death of the Rev. Richard Fally Cleveland.

1854 Grover Cleveland employed at the Institution for the Blind, 9th Avenue, New York.

1855 Grover Cleveland arrives in Buffalo.

1859 May. Called to the Bar.

1860 Nov. 6th. Election of President Lincoln.

1861 Feb. 4th. Southern States form Confederacy.

1861 April. Kentucky, North Carolina, Virginia, Tennessee, and Missouri protest against coercion of Confederate States.
April 13th. Fort Sumpter taken by Confederates.

1865 April 9th. Confederates surrender at Appomattox Courthouse.

1870 Cleveland elected Sheriff of Erie County.

1873 Cleveland returns to practice at the Bar.

1875 The Resumption Act passed.

1876 Disputed Presidential Election, Tilden and Hayes.

1878 Bland Silver Bill passed.

1879 Jan. 1st. Cash payments resumed.

1880 Garfield elected President.
Reaction in both parties against the Machine.

1881 Nov. Cleveland elected Mayor of Buffalo.

1882 Nov. Cleveland elected Governor of New York.

1884 Nov. Cleveland elected President of the United States.

1885 March 4th. Inaugural Address.

1886 June 2nd.   President Cleveland married to Miss Folsom.

1887 Dec.   Tariff message.

1888 April.   Fishery Treaty sent to Senate.

Aug.   Retaliation Message.

Nov.   Benjamin Harrison elected President.

1889 April 27th.   Speech at New York Democratic Club.

1890 July 12th.   Sherman Act.

Oct. 1st.   McKinley Act.

1890 Nov.   Republican Defeat at Election of 52nd Congress.

1891 Feb. 10th.   Cleveland's Letter on Free Coinage of Silver.

1892 Nov.   Cleveland elected President, 2nd term.

1893 Jan. 16th.   Revolution in Hawaii.

March.   Cleveland withdraws from Senate Treaty for Annexation of Hawaii.

1893 May.   Monetary Crisis.

Aug. 7th.   Extra Session of Congress.

Nov. 1st.   Sherman Act repealed.

1894 Aug. 27th.   Wilson Act.

1895 May 1st.   English occupy Corinto.

Dec. 17th.   Venezuela Message.

1896 May 28th.   Veto of Harbour and Canal Bill.

June 17th.   President's appeal to Democrats to resist Free Coinage.

July 10th.   Mr. W. G. Bryan nominated for the Presidency.

GROVER CLEVELAND

——◇——

CHAPTER I.

ANCESTRY AND EARLY LIFE.

Birth and Parentage—The Cleveland Family—Settlement of Richard
Cleveland in New York State—Characteristics of Western New
York—First employment of Grover—Death of his Father—
Engagement at a Blind Asylum—Start Westward—Uncle at Buffalo
—The *American Short-horn Herd Book*—Called to the Bar 1859
—Assistant District Attorney 1863—Partner in Laning, Cleveland,
and Folsom—Sheriff of Erie County 1870—Mayor of Buffalo 1882.

GROVER CLEVELAND is the son of a Presbyterian
clergyman, who at one time had charge of a
congregation at Caldwell in New Jersey. There, on the
18th March, 1837, the future President of the United
States was born, the fifth child given to the care of the
pastor and his wife Anne Neale. The name chosen by
his parents was Stephen Grover, the second name having
been conferred on him in honour of a Mr. Grover, who
was the immediate predecessor of his father in the
ministry at Caldwell. From early years he has always
signed "Grover Cleveland," and it is under this name
he became known to the public.

In all the authorized biographies considerable stress is laid on the fact that his mother was of Irish descent, rejoicing, as she certainly did, in a distinctly Irish name. Her father was a prosperous bookseller at Baltimore; but beyond the circumstances mentioned by Mr. Hensel, that her mother was of German race, by name Real, and a member of the Society of Friends, I have not been able to find any details concerning the President's maternal lineage. Of the Clevelands we have the account similar in outline to that generally given in the family histories of many celebrated American statesmen. There is the legend of origin in some part of the British Islands. We catch glimpses of the stock as pioneers in the West or as professional men in the larger towns, and there is often some connection of a grandfather or a great-grandfather with the heroic times of the Republic, either through personal service in the struggle for independence or association with the eminent men who took part in it. The same features may be discerned in the ancestry of Webster, Clay, Fillmore, Zachary Taylor, and others. The Clevelands are supposed to have come from England early in the 17th century, and to have settled in Connecticut,—a State of limited area, but famous in the annals of New England.

The link with the historic past is supplied in the person of Dr. Aaron Cleveland, the grandfather of the President's grandfather. Aaron was an Episcopal minister at Philadelphia and a friend of Benjamin Franklin, and his death is recorded in eulogistic terms by the latter in the *Pennsylvania Gazette* of 1757. A descendant of this Aaron took an active part in the Connecticut legislature;

and subsequently, members of the family are heard of as silversmiths, or lawyers, or clergymen. They are engaged in various callings, all showing a strong bend towards mental work, whether in Connecticut, in Vermont, in New York, or other States. The migratory habits of the time are conspicuous when any attempt is made to trace these family histories. What is chiefly remarkable in the Cleveland records is the aptitude for intellectual activity and the variety of forms in which this was exhibited. Politics and the clerical profession seem to have alternately attracted the most capable representatives of the family. The disposition to preach the Gospel was not permanently associated with any special creed, as we should find, for instance, among the dissenters in England. The descendants of Aaron became distinguished pastors of the Congregationalists or the Presbyterians, or reverted to the old Episcopal opinions of their most distinguished representative in the last century. Here we have again an illustration of the detachment from those hereditary lines which prevail in old-world societies.

The father of Mr. Cleveland was a graduate of Yale. He ministered to various congregations in several of the Middle States, and a few years after the birth of his fifth child migrated to Fayetteville, a rising town in the State of New York. From 1841 the Clevelands have been connected with this vast prosperous community, and it was as a citizen of New York State that Mr. Cleveland first appeared in public life.

After nine years at Fayetteville the Rev. Richard Fally Cleveland removed to Clinton in Oneida County, and in

1853 there was another change to Holland Patent on the Black River, a village 15 miles from Utica.

Other children followed ; and the education of four boys and five girls was no light charge on the resources of a country clergyman. It was at the villages of Fayetteville and Clinton that Grover spent those eventful years of school life which mould the character of the future man. With the exception of a year in New York City, immediately after his father's death, the whole of the private life of young Cleveland was passed in this region, which, although it is a part of New York, in geographical position and economic development has a history of its own, more distinctly marked, perhaps, than that of many States. Situated beyond the watershed of the Hudson, it belongs to the basin of Lake Ontario, and constitutes a district enjoying many advantages from the richness of its soil and its proximity to the water system of the Great Lakes. Lying north of the Helderberg Mountains, and west of the romantic Adirondacks, it extends some three hundred miles from the Mohawk valley to the shores of Lakes Ontario and Erie.

The natural resources of the Ontario slope were soon multiplied by the triumphs of engineering which brought it into relation with the commercial enterprise of the seaports. The Erie canal linked the Lakes with the shipping of New York Bay, and later on the extension of railways studded the plains with considerable trading towns. Buffalo, Rochester, Syracuse, Utica, Ithaca, are some of the great communities which were growing up in that region whilst the Rev. Fally Cleveland was struggling with the cares of his increasing family in the various agricultural villages to which his ministry called him. Accordingly, although young Cleveland lived a rural life as a boy, it was a life pulsating with the commercial energy which was then active from the Hudson all along the Mohawk and the Genesee as far as the shores of the Lakes.

As the household grew in numbers, it became necessary to find employment for the elder boys. The young Grover returned when 14 years of age from Clinton to Fayetteville to make his first experience of practical work, being appointed a clerk or salesman in the village store at a salary of 50 dollars the first year, and 100 dollars the second. This start in the business of life is not suggestive of adventure, as were the earlier years of Jackson or Lincoln. The career of Mr. Cleveland brings us to a widely different period of American history,—much more diverse than the dates alone would lead us to expect.

Such a beginning of the struggle for subsistence has not the romantic simplicity which one associates with the youth of Webster, passed amidst the remains of Indian encampments, or of Garfield, a boat driver on a canal in Ohio. Both these celebrated men experienced in different localities what Mr. Phelps calls "the poverty of the frontier," and acquired that aptness of resource and freedom from routine which flourish in new settlements. Cleveland's experience was of a different kind, more suited, perhaps, to lay the foundations of useful work at a period when the growth of population and the pressure of industrial rivalry present an entirely new series of problems. From the village school he passed to the village shop ; not an inappropriate training for the statesman whose work was to be done in the era of peace and commercial progress that followed on the Civil War. This first practical business, concerned with small retail transactions in the general store of a rural district, was the preparation for those studies which have made Mr. Cleveland the arbitrator between the various tariff and currency parties, between the capitalists and manufacturers of the Eastern States and the small farmer and store-keeper of the agricultural States in the wide West.

Before he had completed two years in this humble situation, his father called him home in the hope of carrying out arrangements to secure him a University education; but he had made little progress with his new course of studies when death cut off Richard Fally Cleveland, and further educational schemes had to be postponed in order to enable the elder children to aid in the support of the widow and the younger members of the family.

His elder brother, William, was already engaged as a teacher in the Institution for the Blind in New York, and here he was able to find a place for Grover as a clerk and book-keeper at a considerable advance on the salary he had been receiving in the country store. An anecdote is related of him which shows, at this early age, the sturdy character lying beneath his patient exterior and unobtrusive manner. Stricken with sorrow, a stranger in a great city, the rustic lad attracted the sympathy of a pupil teacher in the Institution older than himself. She shared his taste for poetry, and he read her passages from Moore and Byron when opportunity allowed. On one occasion she asked him to copy out one of these poems; the manager of the Institution coming into his office found him engaged

in copying under Miss Crosby's direction, and at once said
to her, "When you want Mr. Cleveland to copy a piece for
you I will thank you to come and ask me." As soon as
the superintendent left, young Cleveland pointed out to
his friend that she ought not to submit passively to be
lectured in that way, and arranged with her to make him
a similar request the following day, when she would be
prepared to reprove her critic. The meddlesome official
was again on the alert, but rebuked for his interference;
he never returned to the subject.*

After a year's stay in New York, Cleveland made up his
mind to follow the movement which was then in full vigour,
and join the stream of settlers who were migrating from
the East into the Western States. The rising city of
Cleveland, in Ohio, was his goal, and, accompanied by a
friend also bent on making his way in the newer States,
he left New York in 1855. After a visit to his mother at
Holland Patent he pushed on to Buffalo, then the most
progressive of the cities in this flourishing region of the
great Lakes. This community numbered some 4000 at
the beginning of the century, and now claims a population
of 255,000.

Here dwelt an uncle of Cleveland's, named Allen; and
the young men called to see him on their journey west.
Apparently, there was no thought at first of finding any
occupation for the lad of seventeen in this bustling locality.
Mr. Allen owned a large farm on an island in the Niagara
River, and was celebrated as a breeder of short-horns.
He was at this time preparing, in connection with his
business, a descriptive catalogue called the *American*

* *Life of Grover Cleveland*, by G. F. PARKER, p. 18.

Short-horn Herd Book. Struck with the intelligence of his nephew, he proposed that Cleveland should suspend his scheme of seeking employment among strangers, and devote some time to helping him with this book.

After some months' labour bestowed on the Herd Book, an opportunity arose for getting young Cleveland into a lawyer's office, and this was readily embraced, for the legal profession had been the boy's ambition.

In his new position he succeeded so well that by the end of the year he was permanently engaged by the firm of Messrs. Brown and Rogers.

It was at work in their chambers that he laid the foundation of those great legal acquirements which placed him at the head of his profession before his election to high position in the Government. In 1857 he was called to the bar, and, following the American custom, entered into partnership with other members of the profession.

To his first arrival in Buffalo he referred, in subsequent years, when a candidate for the Governorship of New York State.

"I can but remember to-night the time when I came among you friendless, unknown, and poor; I can but remember how step by step, by the encouragement of my good fellow citizens, I have gone on to receive more of their appreciation than is my due, until I have been honoured with more distinction than I deserve."

He was appointed in 1863 assistant District Attorney for the county of Erie, the county in which Buffalo is situated, and at the expiration of his period of employment he entered into partnership with a law firm under the style of Laning, Cleveland, and Folsom. In 1870 his friends persuaded him to stand for the office of Sheriff, a request which he hesitated to accept, as his practice had become very remunerative; but three years' tenure of this office gave him a useful knowledge of general affairs, and on his return to private professional practice his income became larger than ever. He was the head of the firm of Cleveland, Bissell, and Sicard, when he was elected Governor of New York in 1882.

His success at the bar was due to his grasp of facts and lucidity of statement, not to any display of rhetoric. From the first, his reputation was that of a man of great vigour and industry, whose knowledge and uprightness won the respect of the judges and of his own profession. He was too well employed to take an active part in politics; and, indeed, it is not the custom in the Union for the industrious or orderly to join in the turmoil of public meetings. These are left to the professional politicians and their satellites. But Mr. Cleveland, we learn, was always ready to do such share of public work as the habits of his country, and his professional occupation, made possible. On election days he regularly assisted in distributing the ballot papers. He paid his subscription to the party funds, and took his place in the customary demonstrations. Twice he had received local nominations, standing as District Attorney for Erie County in 1865, when he was unsuccessful, and being elected Sheriff in 1870. But these appointments, although they were made by a popular vote, were to posts connected with his professional work; and it was only when he was elected, ten years afterwards, Mayor of Buffalo, that he can be said to have really applied himself to public matters. Up to that time he was an active member of the community, gaining every day in wealth, influence, and consideration among his countrymen, but never showing the slightest eagerness for political distinction. Although he was already connected with one of the great political parties and had twice held professional offices, his public career may be said to have practically begun with his nomination as Mayor of the city of Buffalo in October, 1881. He was the nominee of the Democratic party, and although the other city officers chosen at the same election were Republicans, he was elected by an overwhelming majority. His success was no party triumph, but the tribute paid by his fellow townsmen to his abilities and uprightness of character.

CHAPTER II.

MAYORALTY OF BUFFALO.

The American city—Similarity of institutions in City, State and
Union—The veto power—The Mayor and the Street Commissioner's
buggy—The "Plain Speech Veto"—The Sewer Commission—
Decoration Day—Cleveland candidate for the Governorship of
New York—Republican support.

THE term "city" in America means what we should
describe as a municipality. It is a community organized with certain powers of taxation and justice within
the area of the State, and the definition of the authority
conceded to it is called a charter. This incorporating act
may be either special or general, as in England, but the
effect of either is practically the same. We have a
microcosm of the State in each city government, very
much as the modern State constitution is a microcosm of
the Federal constitution of 1787. There is in all three cases
a widely extended suffrage : sometimes the franchise in the
city or state is more liberal in one locality than in another.
Many states and cities admit aliens to the polls before
they have completed the period of residence necessary to
make them citizens of the United States, in the international meaning of the term ; and admission to the
suffrage in the State involves admission to vote at Federal
elections. In all three cases we have a similar outline in

the distribution of public powers,—a popular representative body whose consent is necessary to the imposition of taxes, and passing of laws, and a controlling executive elected also by the constituency, and possessing some form of veto on nearly every act of the representative assemblies. The functionary exercising the veto, whether he be called Mayor, Governor, or President, is the personal expression of popular authority in restraint of the representatives of the people. In the case of most cities the representative body is known by the old English name of Common Council.

The functions of the Mayor are of two kinds. He is authorized to give certain advice and make suggestions to the Council, whilst by-laws cannot be passed, rates levied, or expenditure legalized without his consent.

It was Mr. Cleveland's vigorous use of his veto power against the Common Council of Buffalo which first attracted attention, at a time when complaints of jobbery were heard from nearly every city in the Eastern States. The waste and corruption found in the government of cities have been acknowledged by Americans of all parties. These evils are worse in the older cities; but the towns of more recent origin, like Buffalo, have not escaped them.

The new Mayor, in his inaugural address to the City Council, lays down one or two principles which the reader might be inclined to regard as truisms, but which appear to have been truths neglected in the lake city.

" We hold the money of the people in our hands, to be used for their purposes and to further their interests as members of the municipality, and it is quite apparent that when any part of the funds which the taxpayers have thus entrusted to us is devoted to other purposes, or when by design or neglect we allow a greater sum to be applied to any municipal purpose than is necessary, we have to that extent violated our duty. There surely is no difference in his duties and obligations, whether a person is entrusted with the money of one man or many; and yet it sometimes appears as though the office holder assumes that a different rule of fidelity prevails between him and the taxpayers than that which should regulate his conduct when, as an individual, he holds the money of his neighbours."

The theory that public administration should be conducted for the most part on the same principles which would guide an intelligent business man in the conduct of his own affairs, recurs over and over again in the official documents issued by Mr. Cleveland, whether as Mayor of Buffalo, Governor of the State, or President of the Republic.

In his first message he called attention to the discreditable condition of the streets. "The recent investigation into the affairs of this Department," he bluntly says, "has developed the most shameful neglect of duty on the part of the persons in charge." He goes on to point out that the business of the Street Commissioner is "to superintend" the various works carried on. "This superintendence means something more than certifying accounts, when presented, without any examination." Even of the accounts there was no proper record. The construction of the side-walks cost nearly 50 per cent. more than the charge for similar work done for private persons. On the other hand, the contract for cleaning the streets was fixed at a very low price, and no steps were taken to see that the work paid for was actually done.

"We should pay for the work," said the Mayor, "what it is reasonably worth, and a contract once entered into should be rigidly enforced." As regards the inspectors who should assist the Street Commissioner, he declared that the persons appointed frequently either had no idea of a proper performance of their duties, or were incapable of doing the work required of them. The closing of the city offices at 4 o'clock, whilst ordinary business premises were kept open much later, was another practice which he condemned. He urged that the convenience of all citizens should be consulted in respect of the hours during which the offices should remain open.

With the Street Commissioner the Mayor had a prolonged struggle, which illustrates the exercise of the veto power, and affords a glimpse of ordinary municipal administration.

Early in April, 1882, an account came in and was sanctioned by the Council, allowing the Commissioner $75 for the keep of a horse and buggy during the previous quarter. Mr. Cleveland pointed out that the Charter of the city granted by the State Legislature expressly prohibited incidental additions to the income of public officers. The Commissioner had undertaken to do certain duties at a fixed salary. In this particular case there was the further objection that, previous to his appointment, some such allowance had been suggested and the Council had refused it.

"If the discharge of these duties involve the necessity of using and keeping a horse, that expense should be regarded, as it seems to me, as incidental only to the proper discharge of such duty, and there can be no valid claim for reimbursement against the city. The salary is the measure of compensation for all the duties which the officer is required to perform, and can no more be increased by the allowance of a yearly sum for the use of a horse and wagon than of a yearly sum for the wages of a servant attached to his person."*

In May of the same year the account came in again, was a second time passed by the Council, and again vetoed. In October the Council passed a warrant in favour of a Mr. Denis Danahy for a sum of $99, at $3 a day for "transportation." It appeared on enquiry that "transportation" meant the carrying the Commissioner from place to place, and that the carrying was done by the identical horse and buggy referred to on previous occasions, which the Commissioner had since sold to his kinsman Mr. Danahy. Thus the original claim of $300 a year was run up in a new form to $1000, and it further appeared, in the course of the discussion, that the equipage had been the gift to the Commissioner from the inspecting staff, who were subject to him in the discharge of their duties.

Another practice of the pre-Cleveland time was the frequency of liberal payments to the press. The Charter prescribed the maintenance of an official record, and the rule had been for the party who happened to have a majority in the Council to make a handsome allowance, under this head, to the chief newspaper on their side. Although this was an expenditure over which he had no veto, Mr. Cleveland urged that it ought not to be treated as "a proffered reward for party service, or an item of political patronage," and suggested that the Council should advertise for tenders.

* *Life of Grover Cleveland*, by PENDLETON KING, p. 39.

Later on a warrant was passed granting $800 a year each to three German papers, on condition of their publishing a synopsis of the Council's proceedings. The plea for this bargain was that many of the taxpayers were only able to read German, and at the head of the list was the German Democratic organ.

This vote Mr. Cleveland at once condemned. He objected to an official report prepared by the clerk, as a questionable innovation. In his opinion the Germans would probably better get all the information they stood in need of through conversation with people who were able to read the official paper.

" The German newspapers mentioned in the resolution depend for their success upon the amount and value of the news or information they furnish to their patrons. We will assume that some account of the proceedings of the Common Council—in other words that a synopsis of such proceedings—is of importance and interest to their readers. I am quite sure that we may safely calculate that from motives of self-interest the proprietors of these newspapers will publish a synopsis much more satisfactory to their subscribers than any which the City Clerk would be able to prepare, and they would do so for their own profit, and without any compensation from the city. If this is true, the effect of the resolution under consideration is to give these newspapers eight hundred dollars each for doing no more than they will in a sense be obliged to do without it. This comes very near being a most objectionable subsidy, which, I think, a little reflection will satisfy us all we ought not to encourage, and which, I am sure, the people are not prepared to tolerate."*

The most celebrated of Mr. Cleveland's Buffalo messages was that known as "the Plain Speech Veto." The Council

* *Life of Grover Cleveland*, by PENDLETON KING, p. 31.

resolved to pay one Talbot, for street cleaning during five years, the sum of $422,500. On this resolution the Mayor thus commented :—

"The bid thus accepted by your honourable body is more than one hundred thousand dollars higher than that of another perfectly responsible party for the same work ; and a worse and more suspicious feature in the transaction is that the bid now accepted is fifty thousand dollars more than that made by Talbot himself within a very few weeks, openly and publicly, to your honourable body, for performing precisely the same services. This latter circumstance is, to my mind, the manifestation on the part of the contractor of a reliance upon the forbearance and generosity of your honourable body, which would be more creditable if it were less expensive to the taxpayers.

"I am not aware that any excuse is offered for the acceptance of this proposal thus increased, except the very flimsy one that the lower bidders cannot afford to do the work for the sums they name.

"This extreme tenderness and consideration for those who desire to contract with the city, and this touching and paternal solicitude lest they should be improvidently led into a bad bargain is, I am sure, an exception to general business rules, and seems to have no place in this selfish, sordid world, except as found in the administration of municipal affairs. . . . .

"This is a time for plain speech, and my objection to the action of your honourable body, now under consideration, shall be plainly stated. I withhold my assent from the same because I regard it as the culmination of a most barefaced, impudent, and shameless scheme to betray the interests of the people, and worse than to squander the public money.

"I will not be misunderstood in this matter. There are those whose votes were given for this resolution whom I cannot and will not suspect of a wilful neglect of the interests they are sworn to protect, but it has been fully demonstrated that there are influences, both in and about your honourable body, which it behoves every honest man to watch and avoid with the greatest care."*

One of the most characteristic examples of Mr. Cleveland's method of administration is supplied by the controversy over the construction of the main sewer in Buffalo. This scheme had been so long postponed that serious mischief to public health had resulted from the condition of the canal running through the lower portion of the city. Mr. Cleveland urged in his opening message that further delay was impossible. Even the question of cost was not admissible except so far as obliging all concerned in the undertaking to seek the cheapest effectual plan. To this appeal the Council assented, and the following month he proposed the appointment of a Commission to carry out the work. The undertaking could not be completed for three years, and it was important to have it commenced and brought to a termination under the same management. The City Engineer was immediately up in arms. He contended that his department was fully qualified and would carry out the business the most economically; neither did the Council sympathize with the proposal to call in the non-office-holding portion of the community. Such an idea practically involved the setting aside the regular machinery of party politics and popular elections. The Mayor answered that the Engineer and his staff would have plenty to do in watching the work as it proceeded and reporting on it to the Council : that they could not be called away from their present occupations so as to devote all the time required for this great enterprise.

The public took up the scheme of the Mayor, and after

* *Life of Grover Cleveland*, by PENDLETON KING, p. 64.

a long struggle an act was passed at Albany authorizing him, subject to confirmation by the Council, to appoint a Commission of five with full power to make contracts and issue bonds. The act was passed on June 8th, and on the 12th the Mayor sent up the names of his Commissioners. By a majority of two the Council refused confirmation. Mr. Cleveland waited a week, and then sent a message pointing out that, in view of the passing of the act, he had devoted much time and thought to the selection of the Commissioners. He referred to the character and standing of these gentlemen, and their entire freedom from any inclination to enrich contractors at the expense of the people, and suggested that their rejection must be due to haste and confusion. With the vacation of the Council at hand, he added, there was no sufficient interval to form another list, and thus much valuable time would be lost. "I am convinced that a majority of your honourable body do not care to be chargeable with this result." This veiled menace was not without effect. The former list, again submitted, was adopted by a large majority.

One other incident of his Mayoralty deserves notice, for it marks the frank resolution with which, all through his career, he has faced those questions connected with the Civil War, which would have been embarrassing to a less manly nature.

The Common Council proposed to pay 500 dollars from a fund connected with the Fire Brigade, as a contribution to the cost of celebrating Decoration Day,—a day devoted in the Northern States to the memory of the men who fell in the Civil War. This proposal Mr. Cleveland determined to veto; and when we recollect that he was presiding over a great Northern community, and was a member of a party who had been the political allies of the men who had fought the Grand Army of the Republic, we can form some estimate of the straightforwardness for which Mr. Cleveland has become famous.

After reciting the vote of the Council and the provisions of the State constitution, he went on to examine the resolution.

"It seems to me that it is not only obnoxious to the provisions of the Constitution above quoted, but that it also violates that section of the charter of the city which makes it a misdemeanour to appropriate money raised for one purpose to any other object. Under this section I think money raised 'for the celebration of the Fourth of July and the reception of distinguished persons,' cannot be devoted to the observance of Decoration Day.

"I deem the object of this appropriation a most worthy one. The efforts of our veteran soldiers to keep alive the memory of their fallen comrades certainly deserve the aid and encouragement of their fellow-citizens. We should all, I think, feel it a duty and a privilege to contribute to the funds necessary to carry out such a purpose. And I should be much disappointed if an appeal to our citizens for voluntary subscriptions for this patriotic object should be in vain.

"But the money so contributed should be a free gift of the citizens and taxpayers, and should not be extorted from them by taxation. This is so, because the purpose for which this money is asked does not involve their protection or interest as members of the community, and it may or may not be approved by them.

"The people are forced to pay taxes into the city treasury only upon the theory that such money shall be expended for public purposes, or purposes in which they all have a direct and practical interest."*

* *Life of Grover Cleveland*, by PENDLETON KING, p. 47.

The administration of the city of Buffalo is in many respects the most interesting part of Mr. Cleveland's career. We see a vigorous, if somewhat primitive, system of government at its best : a strong, energetic man exercising without hesitation the large powers given him by the law, and a community who loyally support him in his struggle with corrupt officials. The capacity shown by the Mayor of Buffalo soon convinced the public that such rare qualities ought to be given a larger sphere of exercise.

In 1882 there was an important crisis in the affairs of the State. The Republicans had for several years been predominant, and in Mr. Cornell had found a Governor who put public duty before party intrigue. His enmity to jobs, however, and indifference to political considerations, did not commend him to the confidence of party "workers." They determined to guard against his nomination for a second term by securing another candidate whose views would be more in accordance with party traditions ; and they selected Mr. Folger, a New York man, who at this time enjoyed the great position of Secretary of the Treasury to President Arthur. This proceeding exposed the Republicans to a double reproach. They showed their indifference to the pressing question of reform in administration by sacrificing an able and upright Governor to the animosity which his public spirit had evoked, and they were accused of seeking to overbear opposition by adopting a great official of the Central Government. The Democrats were not slow to take advantage of such an opportunity. Both New York and Brooklyn announced

candidates in opposition to Mr. Folger ;* but when the
State Convention of the party met at Syracuse, in September, they found that Western New York had a candidate
of its own. Mr. Cleveland's success as Mayor of Buffalo
had determined his fellow townsmen and neighbours to
claim for the Ontario basin the recognition which the
State had not previously accorded to this part of the
country.

To this movement Mr. Cleveland had given no direct
encouragement ; but he was not indisposed to aid his party,
who were perplexed between the rival claims of Mr. Flower
and General Slocum. Mr. Manning was at that time the
head of the New York County Democracy, and the day
before the convention opened it was arranged that Mr.
Cleveland should be invited to Syracuse to see the party
chief. He consented to make an evening visit after his
official day's work was done, traversed the short distance,
and saw Mr. Manning, returning to Buffalo the same night.
The next morning he was nominated as the candidate of
the Democratic party. His proposer, after a eulogy on his
career, described him "as a man who can command not
only the votes of his own party, but also a large proportion of the independent voters of the State," and he was
accepted on the third ballot. The result was a contest of
singular animation.

* Roswell P. Flower was a popular representative of the Democratic organization in New York City, whilst General B. Slocum, of
Brooklyn, who had done distinguished service in the field, boasted
the confidence of the County Democracy.

CHAPTER III.

GOVERNORSHIP OF NEW YORK.

Contest with Folger—Non-Partisan character of Cleveland's address
—Enormous majority for Cleveland—Work at Albany—Important
functions of Governor—More Vetoes—The 5 cent Fare Bill—
Appointments in New York City—A Presidential candidate.

PERSONALLY, Mr. Folger had many claims on the
confidence of his neighbours. He had held an
eminent position on the bench, before he undertook the
high office of Secretary of the Treasury. This post is one
scarcely inferior in importance to that of the President.
The Secretary of the Treasury is nominated by the
President subject to the approval of the Senate, but he
reports to Congress, not to the President, and it has been
contended that he cannot be removed from office during
a Presidential term without the consent of Congress. As
a candidate for the Governorship, however, he represented
the policy of whitewashing abuses. He was called in
to cover, by his exalted position, the sins of his party;
and the people who had been striving for some reform
in local government determined to resist him at all
costs.

In Mr. Cleveland they found a man whose sturdy fight
against local follies and iniquities had already attracted

notice, and who "had not," as Mr. Parker slyly remarks, "been brought into close relations with the people of the State." He had been attending to his own business, and not mixing in the trade of politics. The interview with Manning on September 21st is the only record of any contact between Cleveland and the owners of the "machine." He was altogether outside the ring of professional politicians, and accordingly the independent party in the State at once gave him hearty support.

Although nominated by the party Convention, Mr. Cleveland had not been among the party "workers." He had never served either on the Council of his city, or on party committees,—in the Assembly or the Senate of his State, at State or National Conventions, or in either of the houses at Washington ; and his public utterances had continued to be of a non-partisan character. He was not, in fact, known to the public as a politician. The detachment of the candidate from party passion was conspicuous in his letter accepting the nomination. There is not an allusion in it to the distinctions between Republicans and Democrats, although several of the general principles familiar to Democratic orators may be traced through its paragraphs. He laid particular stress on the demand for Civil Service Reform, and attacked the existing system of filling the State offices with party workers on the following grounds : the interference of public officials at elections was an aggression on liberty, and it was also a fraud upon the public, if it involved a sacrifice of the time which the Civil servant had undertaken to devote to his duties.

The result of the election in November, 1882, was the

unparalleled majority for Cleveland of 192,800 votes. Of the quarter of a million votes given to him, it is calculated that fully 100,000 were Republican.

According to the Rousseau principle of isolating the capital from the chief centre of wealth, the Governor and the representative bodies of the State meet at Albany, a picturesque city on the Hudson, some 150 miles from New York city ; and it was there, on the 1st January 1883, that Mr. Cleveland entered upon his three years period of office. To mark his theory of Republican simplicity, he proceeded on foot from the mansion of the Governor to the palatial building containing the public offices, and after the ceremony of inauguration was over, set about his work in the Governor's room.*

The post which Mr. Cleveland thus undertook is one of which Europeans find it difficult to realize the precise nature. The existence of the State within the Federal system, retaining many of the attributes of sovereignty, having its own staff of officials working side by side with those of the Federal Government, is the most peculiar feature of American public life.

The reader who is curious on the subject, will find in Mr. Bryce's volumes a lucid exposition of the fact so often overlooked, that, whilst the State is an independent community for many purposes, having, for instance, the control of education, of police—in fact, the protection of liberty and property, with courts of first instance and courts of appeal—at the same time every State is an integral part of the American Republic, whose Government has its own judges, and tax collectors,

* *Life of Grover Cleveland,* by PENDLETON KING, p. 113.

and other Federal officers at work within the State area. The Governor is the popularly-elected watchman of a community, exercising all the functions of a national Government, except so far as certain portions of their authority have been transferred to the Federal Administration.

In New York, this office has been filled by some of the men most famous in American history. Among Mr. Cleveland's predecessors were the two Clintons, Chief Justice Jay, President Van Buren, William Seward, Lincoln's Secretary of State, and Mr. Samuel J. Tilden, who was so near recovering the executive power of the Republic for the Democratic Party in 1877.

The State of New York has always held a foremost place, not only as the site of the chief Atlantic port, but as the commonwealth largest in area and population among the whole of the Eastern States. Lying south of New England, it thus forms a connection with the more balmy regions of New Jersey and Maryland; its interior runs north and west to the Great Lakes, and renders it, in conjunction with the port of New York, the natural commercial emporium of North America south of the Saint Lawrence.

Of the city of New York, Mr. Bryce says: "It is the centre of commerce, the sovereign of finance. But it has no special influence, or power, beyond that of casting a large vote, which is an important factor in determining the 36 Presidential votes of the State." * This is perfectly true, as far as laws and constitutions go; but, for all that, the State, with its great commercial city,

---

* Bryce's *American Commonwealth*, vol. ii. p. 663.

has become a laboratory of influences which, in political life and in economics, have extended over distant parts of the Union. Here is found some link between the formal doctrines of the New England States and the more romantic South; whilst in a community like that of the American Republic, so largely engaged in mercantile pursuits, the State which includes in its area the centre of commerce, has necessarily a degree of ascendancy throughout the nation. The extension of the railway system has not only added to its material wealth, but to its importance as the cradle of various activities.

With a population of six and a-half millions, it has, within the last fifty years, adopted great manufacturing industries in addition to its commercial enterprises. Thus it has become not only the most considerable trading commonwealth within the Union, but a competitor with the manufacturers of Pennsylvania on the one side, and of New England on the other.

The good sense which has ever been so conspicuous a trait of Mr. Cleveland's career, is visible in his first message to the State Assembly at Albany. It is full of excellent maxims of government, and contains some suggestions of practical value; but there is an absence of that imperious tone with which people had become familiar in the Veto Mayor of Buffalo. He recognizes the difference in the much larger sphere to which he has been called, and awaits the light of further experience before seeking to impose his own views on his fellow citizens. One passage is characteristic of his faith in the Democratic principle that responsibility should rest with the head of the administration. Referring to the misgovernment of cities—a topic then familiar to the New York public—he says :

"If, to remedy this evil, the chief executive should be made answerable to the people for the proper conduct of the city affairs, it is quite clear that his power in the selection of those who manage its different departments should be greatly enlarged." *

This advice was adopted in a remarkable act passed for the city of New York the following year.

It was not long before the crop of bills sent up by the Assembly and the Senate, obliged him to assert at Albany those principles of good government which he had maintained with such energy at Buffalo. It has been already † related how in that city he had shown his indifference to partisan reproach by vetoing an appropriation for Decoration Day,—the festival celebrated throughout the Northern States in honour of the soldiers who fell in the Civil War. In Albany, a bill was passed authorizing a County Board to purchase land out of the county rates for the erection of a soldiers' monument. The Governor declared that the object was a worthy and a patriotic one, but, he added :

"I cannot forget that the money proposed to be appropriated is public money, to be raised by taxation, and that all that justifies its exaction from the people is the necessity of its use for purposes connected with the safety and substantial welfare of the taxpayers." ‡

* PENDLETON KING, p. 117.
† See p. 19.
‡ *Cleveland's Writings and Speeches*, 1892, p. 437.

Both at Elmira and in his own city of Buffalo, he found the Democrats eager to turn the triumph of the recent election to party account; but the bills sent up were rejected by the Governor in terms of strong reproof. In regard to the scheme promoted by the Democrats of Buffalo, he said:

"I believe in an open and sturdy partisanship which secures the legitimate advantages of party supremacy; but parties were made for the people. I am unwilling knowingly to give my assent to measures purely partisan, which will sacrifice or endanger their interests."

An upright man, in the position of Governor of New York, has many opportunities of checking, on the one hand, those corrupting influences which powerful corporations are too often able to bring to bear upon a popular organization, and, on the other, of protecting capital against the raids of unscrupulous faction. The Democrats have always been suspicious of wealthy corporations; and Jackson owed his popularity almost as much to his crusade against the Bank of the United States, as to his victory at New Orleans. But honest adherence to public contracts has hitherto been an article of faith with the party: not so much from any clear conception of the value of public credit, as from a manly sense of honour and fair dealing.

It was to these better traditions that Mr. Cleveland appealed when he resisted the attempt to court popularity at the expense of the Manhattan Railway Company. A bill was carried through the Legislature to reduce to five cents all fares between the Battery and Harlem River, a distance of about ten miles. The original charter of the

Company contained a provision that the fare should not exceed five cents per mile. Subsequently additional powers were granted, and the limitation of fare was changed to a maximum of five cents for two miles. Finally the Company were authorized to levy a uniform rate, not exceeding ten cents for the distance from Harlem to the Battery. It was part of the agreement that the Company should pay five per cent. of their income into the city treasury.

These acts, the Governor declared, brought the Company within the protection of that clause of the Constitution of the United States which prohibits the passage of a law by any State impairing the obligation of contracts, and he vetoed the bill in a remarkable message :—

"The fact is notorious that for many years rapid transit was the great need of the city of New York, and was of direct importance to the citizens of the State. Projects which promised to answer the people's wants in this direction failed, and were abandoned. The Legislature, appreciating the situation, willingly passed statute after statute calculated to aid and encourage a solution of the problem. Capital was timid, and hesitated to enter a new field full of risks and dangers. By the promise of liberal fares, as will be seen in all the acts passed on the subject, and through other concessions gladly made, capitalists were induced to invest their money in the enterprise, and rapid transit but lately became an accomplished fact. But much of the risk, expense, and burden attending the maintenance of these roads, are yet unknown and threatening. In the meantime, the people of the city of New York are receiving the full benefit of their construction, a great enhancement of the value of the taxable property of the city has resulted, and in addition to taxes, more than $120,000—being five per cent. in increase—pursuant to the law of 1868, has been paid by the Companies into the city treasury, on the faith that the rate of fare agreed upon was secured to them. I am not aware that the corporations have, by any default, forfeited any of their rights ; and if they have, the remedy is at hand under existing laws. . . . .

" It is manifestly important that invested capital should be protected, and that its necessity and usefulness in the development of enterprises valuable to the people, should be recognized by conservative conduct on the part of the State Government.

" But we have especially in our keeping the honour and good faith of a great State, and we should see to it that no suspicion attaches, through any act of ours, to the fair fame of the commonwealth." *

Whilst he was thus prepared to defend corporations against legislative plunder, he was equally ready to do whatever the Government could in order to protect the small investor from fraud. In his second annual message he defended the inquiries of the newly appointed Railway Commission concerning the management of the Companies.

" The action of the board in requiring the filing of quarterly reports by the railroad companies, exhibiting their financial condition, is a most important step in advance, and should be abundantly sustained. . . . . . The State creates these corporations upon the theory that some proper thing of benefit can be better done by them than by private enterprise, and that the aggregation of the funds of many individuals may be thus profitably employed. They are launched upon the public with the seal of the State in some sense upon them."

Reference has already been made to Mr. Cleveland's observations in his first message as Governor on the evils

---

* *Cleveland's Writings and Speeches*, p. 445.

of "divided responsibility." The principle of individual supremacy which may be traced through every form of political organization in the Union, whether in the Mayor, Governor, or President, is in truth the necessary counterpoise in practice of the doctrines of universal equality laid down in the Declaration of Independence; and it was to this resource that thoughtful men in New York looked to secure permanent results from the reform movement in which Mr. Manning and the County Democracy had taken so active a part for many years past.

Whilst the alterations in the Federal Constitution have been so few, the State Constitutions have been undergoing a continual process of change since the Revolution. In the earlier part of this century the movement was towards the development of the first part of the Jeffersonian theory,—popular election. Latterly these changes have been supplemented by a considerable increase of the Governor's powers. His right of veto, for instance, is recognized as a formal stage in legislation, and bills passed at Albany by large majorities of both Houses are discussed before the Governor in arguments which sometimes extend over several days.

Under the old State Constitution of 1777 there was a Council of Appointment constituted to fill a number of public offices. Of this the Governor was chairman with a casting vote. Then, as Jeffersonian ideas spread through the Union and the suffrage was lowered, nearly every official was chosen by direct election. When the abuses of this system became intolerable, recourse was had to the model set in the Federal Constitution, and the

Governor was empowered to make appointments subject to approval by a representative body, such as, in the State, the Senate, in the City of New York, the Board of Aldermen.

In 1884 the suggestion of Mr. Cleveland, made the previous year, was adopted, and an act passed to provide that all appointments hitherto made by the Mayor, and confirmed by the Board of Aldermen, might henceforth be "made by the Mayor without such confirmation."

Mr. Cleveland determined to sanction this measure, and took advantage of the excitement which had attended the discussion of it to present a vigorous exposition of the theory of personal power derived from universal suffrage. He dealt with the appeals which had been made to him to exercise his veto on the grounds that the bill was an invasion of popular rights, an aggression by the State on the municipality, and continued :—

"If the chief executive of the city is to be held responsible for its order and good government, he should not be hampered by any interference with his selection of subordinate administration officers, nor should he be permitted to find in a divided responsibility an excuse for any neglect of the best interests of the people.

"The plea should never be heard that a bad nomination had been made because it was the only one that could secure confirmation. . . . .

"An absolute and undivided responsibility on the part of the appointing power accords with correct business principles, the application of which to public affairs will always, I believe, direct the way to good administration and the protection of the people's interests.

"The intelligence and watchfulness of the citizens of New York should certainly furnish a safe guarantee that the duties and powers devolved by this legislation upon their chosen representative will be well and wisely bestowed; and if they err or are betrayed, their remedy is close at hand.

"I can hardly realize the unprincipled boldness of the man who would accept at the hands of his neighbours this sacred trust, and standing alone in the full light of public observation should wilfully prostitute his powers and defy the will of the people.

"To say that such a man could by such means perpetuate his wicked rule, concedes either that the people are vile or that self-government is a deplorable failure. . . .

"But the best opportunities will be lost, and the most perfect plan of city government will fail, unless the people recognize their responsibilities and appreciate and re-realize the privileges and duties of citizenship. With the most carefully devised charter, and with all the protection which legislative enactments can afford them, the people of the city of New York will not secure a wise and economical rule until those having the most at stake determine to actively interest themselves in the conduct of municipal affairs."*

This was perhaps the most important question which arose during Mr. Cleveland's second year of office, and his utterance deserves attention not merely as an incident in the history of New York, but as illustrating the principle that the power of the Executive is regarded as a check upon the ignorance and bad faith of legislative bodies. With this policy the Democratic party have been repeatedly identified, and it is one to which the career of Mr. Cleveland has given special prominence.

He was soon concerned with much larger questions. The Reform movement, to which allusion has already been made as pervading for some time local and national politics, was particularly active as the Presidential election

---

* KING's *Cleveland*, p. 161.

of 1884 approached ; and the Democratic party came to
the conclusion that the line of policy which had enabled
them to wrest the government of New York State from
the Republicans, might serve them equally well in the
more important enterprise of securing the control of the
national administration. Mr. Cleveland's resolution, and
his indifference to party and to popularity hunting, had
attracted some attention outside the State, whilst the
approbation he had won within its borders seemed likely
to ensure to the Democratic party the New York vote ;
and this counted 36 out of a total of 401.

On the 28th June, 1884, he consented to be put in
nomination for the Presidency.

CHAPTER IV.

AMERICAN PARTIES.

Choice of party connection—Cleveland joins the Democrats—The oldest of American parties—Influence of Jefferson—The veto power—The Federalists—The Whigs—The Republicans—Composition of parties in 1884.

MR. CLEVELAND, it has been already stated, was a member of the Democratic party. In older countries, the choice of a political connection depends on family, or creed, or class; or perhaps on local circumstances. In the Union, it is more generally a matter of business associations. In the case of the young barrister, there was nothing to attract him specially to one side more than the other. His uncle at Buffalo, who has been already mentioned, Mr. Allen, had long been a member of the Republican party. Among his intimate friends was Judge Tracy, a distinguished lawyer, celebrated in the locality for his public spirit and independence. He had worked first on the Democratic side, and had afterwards become a Whig; but he had refused any official position. His power of mind and varied experience gave him great influence over young men; and it is said that it was in the company of this shrewd political observer that Cleveland acquired the indifference to mere party cries, which has been one of his most striking characteristics.

Dislike of the pretensions and self-seeking of the Republican managers may have had something to do with his adoption of Democratic opinions. Perhaps, too, his vigorous nature led him to select the weakest side, in the hope of restoring them to the position they once held in the Commonwealth, and thus completely effacing the memory of the Civil War.

Before, however, introducing the subject of this memoir as a party politician, some endeavour must be made to give the European reader an idea what party terms in America mean.

It was said of American parties as late as 1889:

"Neither party has any principles, any distinctive tenets. Both have traditions; both claim to have tendencies; both have certainly war cries, organizations, interests enlisted in their support. But those interests are in the main the interests of getting or of keeping the patronage of the Government . . . All has been lost except office or the hope of it."*

This was, in a sense, more accurate in 1889 than it is now, for the policy of Mr. Cleveland has done much to bring into relief those distinctive principles of the Demo-crats which were lost from sight after the War of Secession. Even in England, which may be called the cradle of party organization, the dividing line of thought between one party and another—between Tory and Whig, Con-servative and Liberal—has, at times, become perceptible only to political experts; but the general principles which mark the career of the two great parties in the United States are more distinctly traceable than are the tenets of parties among ourselves. Their final cause is, in fact,

* Bryce's *American Commonwealth*, vol. ii. p. 20.

more easily explained from the nature of American institutions. An examination of their history shows that the filiation of ideas is more complete in the Democratic party than in the case of their great rivals. There is some confusion from change of name, but not more than there is in the early history of party in England from change of dynasty.

In the minds of many there is a vague idea that the Democrats are the friends of the South, who were spared by the magnanimity of the Republicans at the close of the Civil War, and have been since resuscitated by the nation as a means of correcting the sins of power in the Republicans. On the contrary, they are the oldest of the American political organizations, and have had far more to do with the history of the Union than the Republicans.

The present Democratic party are lineally descended from the first opposition which was organized in the Union after the adoption of the Constitution of 1787. During the two presidencies of Washington, the exultation at the great discovery, the Federal Constitution, the cherishing of the new political birth, became the main business of the President and his colleagues. Pride in the infant nation was the dominant feeling; but as to the character of the new nationality and of the Government which should represent it, differences of opinion were, as time went on, developed, and the more rapidly as the events of the French Revolution, and the outbreak of the war between England and France, became known in America.

No one can read over the Declaration of Independence*

* See note to this chapter, p. 54.

adopted in 1776, and the Constitution agreed on in
1787–88, without being struck by the different spirit
which breathes through each of these documents. The
first was, in a great part, the composition of Jefferson;
the second was moulded under the eye of Washington,
whilst Jefferson was in Paris drinking deep of the enthusiasm inspired by the approach of the French Revolution.
It was only at the end of 1789 that Jefferson returned from
France to accept from the first President the post of
Secretary of State. Although he continued in this
position for nearly four years, his passion for the democratic ideas of the French Revolutionists grew warmer,
the greater the reaction he observed in Philadelphia; and
he soon applied himself, although still the Minister of
Washington, and the colleague of Hamilton and Knox,
to organize a party, which, on the new lines of Jacobinism,
should occupy the position so often held in England by
the country party as against the Crown and the Central
Government.

The Constitution of 1787 was a compromise between
the old liberties of the States and the necessities of the
new National Government. The men who thought the
President and his advisers too conservative in their
views, too indifferent to what they regarded as the great
struggle for human advancement going on in France,
somewhat inclined to look with favour on the former
enemy of American liberty—England—aristocratic and
exclusive in their sympathies and bearing, these men
naturally fell back on the State organizations. To develop
the freedom of the masses in these local commonwealths,
to resist the growth of centralization, became their main

objects; and in opposition to the majority in the Federal
Congress, they called themselves Democratic Republicans. They were for the Republic: but it was a Republic
governed by the people, and managed by the people; not
by special sets in Philadelphia, or Boston, or New York.
Accordingly, this new advanced party, who criticised the
President and his Cabinet, who sought to lower the
suffrage in the States, became known as Republicans;
whilst the holders of office were described as Federalists,
or champions of the Federal Union.

Universal suffrage now prevails throughout the Union;
but for nearly two generations, property qualifications
were required for the enjoyment of citizenship in the
older States, and their abolition was mainly due to the
teaching of Jefferson.

The lines of party were already marked when
Washington refused a third term in 1797. From the
time that Jefferson left office, on account of his differences
with Hamilton on the subject of foreign politics, he
devoted all his energies to the propagation of democratic
ideas. They had found expression in the Declaration
of Independence, and had become more fervid as he
contemplated the course of the French Revolution and
the struggle between England and France. Whilst the
subtle imagination of Hamilton was developing the plan
of a National Government, which should combine the
stability and effectiveness of a Monarchy with the
freedom and simplicity of a rustic Republic, Jefferson
was arguing out conclusions from his principles of universal equality.

He was not moved by the reaction which the massacres

of the French Revolution produced. Referring to those dire events, he wrote, " Were there an Adam and an Eve left in every country, and left free, it would be better than it is now." Defeated by John Adams in the election of 1797, he exerted his brilliant powers to oppose the anti-revolutionary policy of the new President. The Alien and Sedition Laws, and other coercive measures, which Adams and Hamilton declared to be necessary in order to save the Union from becoming involved in the whirlpool of the Revolution, he denounced with passion. His draft of the Kentucky Resolutions of 1798 practically involved the principle of secession.

It was the heat of the controversy over the great European War that gave American parties their external shape; but the main characteristics of each are suggested by that dual structure of government, which Mr. Bryce has so admirably described. A knowledge of this system is the first condition for any comprehension of American politics. The primary business of the two parties is to maintain, the one the right of the State, the other the efficiency of the Central Government. Accordingly the Democrats contended that the Constitution which created the Union must be interpreted strictly: that the Federal Government could exercise no authority whatever not expressly conceded by the Constitution. The Federalists, on the other hand, argued that this document should be construed liberally: that the duties assigned to the National Government implied the existence of many powers not distinctly enumerated. Public works, the Democratic Republicans maintained, should be carried out by the States, not by the Union; and they waged perpetual war on the principle of one national bank as tending to promote centralization. They were against centralization, against any control by the money power, and ultimately against protection.

Fortunately, perhaps, for the world, the French revolutionary movement had lost some of its popularity before the accession of the Democratic Republican party to office in 1800. Jacobinical theories in Europe had already made way for Cæsarism in practice, and Jefferson contented himself with reducing the navy, which had been constructed as a menace to France. One of his achievements in office was the sweeping away of such remnants of ceremonial as Washington had retained.

For the next twenty-four years, the Democratic party held uninterrupted sway, and the Federalists practically died out. But this long tenure of power did not seriously affect the strength of the Federal tie. However strong an advocate of local liberty any President may have been in his previous career, in office he necessarily becomes more or less of a Federalist.

It is with the teaching of Jefferson that the Democratic party have been mainly concerned, and his ideas have exercised a much more permanent and a wider influence on American affairs than any other statesman can claim. The achievements of Washington were, perhaps, the condition of the existence of the Union; but he dealt with practical questions as they arose. He was a soldier, not a theorist; whilst Jefferson was not only a statesman, but, according to his lights, a philosopher. In the Declaration of Independence, he provided a political catechism for the whole nation.

The commentary on the Declaration of Independence is found in the Jefferson correspondence. He writes to President Washington : * " I am convinced that those societies like the Indians, who live without government, enjoy in their general mass an infinitely greater degree of happiness than those who live under European governments." Again, he says, " A little rebellion now and then is a good thing." †

It would be a mistake, however, to suppose, from these phrases, that this remarkable man had any sympathy with anarchy. It was against the danger of a Central Government, against the development of a political class, that his efforts were directed. The theory of universal equality, which he had inserted in the Declaration of Independence, was the principle to which he clung.

In that document the tyranny of George III. is the main theme : but the statesmen assembled at Philadelphia and the leaders of the Revolution were sufficiently well informed to know that it was a political class who were their opponents, not a despot ; and underlying the whole of the speeches of this time, and the principles adopted in their constitutions, is the profound antipathy to such a class. Their rooted purpose was to provide against the growth of a privileged order in the new Commonwealth. When Jefferson is denouncing the Bank, it is not a despotism that he fears from it. " It will be the instrument for producing a King, Lords, and Commons." ‡ It is not Monarchy so much as the train

---

* *Jefferson's Works*, vol. ii. p. 100.
† *Ibid.* p. 105.
‡ *Ibid.* vol. iii. p. 362.

that attends on Monarchy, which the fathers of the Republic have in view. It is not so much liberty in the abstract at which they aim, as the abolition of class distinctions.

Jefferson has given us his view of how the principle of equality should be worked out. His ideal, he tells us, is a country "where every man is a sharer in the direction of his ward-republic, or of some of the higher ones; and feels that he is a participator in the government of affairs, not merely at an election one day in the year, but every day, where there shall not be a man in the State who will not be a member of some one of its councils, great or small." *

It is a curious illustration of the vanity of human wishes, that the nation who have made it their special object to pursue equality, and bring political power within the reach of everyone, have evolved the most perfect example of the professional politician which the world has yet seen.

Graphic descriptions have made the public familiar with the "boss"; but it is sometimes forgotten that in many of the States his income, at least during the earlier stages of his career, is provided for out of the taxes. The elections are conducted by public officials chosen in equal numbers from the two party organizations, the theory of legislation being that party spirit will make each set a check upon the other. For the pay of these temporary election officers, Mr. Ivins calculated some years ago that New York City contributes out of the rates on an average £55,000 a year. †

* *Jefferson's Works*, vi. 543 (607).
† *Scribner's Magazine*, February, 1888.

Jefferson and his followers did not foresee that in their antipathy to a privileged body of citizens they were preparing the way for the establishment of the machine ; but as practical men, acquainted with administration, they felt that a necessary counterpart of their principle of equality was some form of the one-man power. The model for it existed, as Mr. Bryce points out, in the authority of the governors under the old Colonial Constitutions ; but it was, in fact, the indispensable palliative of what appears to older nations to be the phantasies of the Declaration of Independence, and it has grown in public estimation in spite of encroachments on the part of Congress.*

The present tendency to increase the influence of the Mayor and Governor, is the effort of practical men to provide for public order in a society organized on Jacobinical principles. Elected by the whole people, and for a limited time, he claims, as Governor Hoffman said, to be "the people's Prime Minister." In order to guard against the devices of politicians, he is clothed with some of the functions of the early tribunes in the Roman Republic. The right of veto has become the main distinction of his office.

The loftiest conception of this individual power is to be found in the speech of Mr. Cleveland towards the end of his first term of office :

"Familiarity with the great office which I hold has but added to my apprehension of its sacred character, and the consecration demanded of him who assumes its

---

* The history of the word "Executive" indicates this development. It has become a personal noun of the singular number.

immense responsibilities. It is the repository of the people's will and power. Within its vision should be the protection and welfare of the humblest citizen, and with quick ear it should catch from the remotest corner of the land the plea of the people for justice and for right. For the sake of the people, he who holds this office of theirs should resist every encroachment upon its legitimate functions; and for the sake of the integrity and usefulness of the office, it should be kept near the people, and be administered in full sympathy with their wants and needs."*

So completely has the delegate politician, as evolved under the American system, forfeited public confidence, that the veto power—purely negative though it be, and liable to be over-ruled by a majority of two-thirds in both Chambers—has come to be regarded as the shield of the people against the predatory enterprises of their representatives. The energy with which Jackson over-ruled Congress contributed almost as much to his popularity as the fact that he had repulsed the English attack on New Orleans, or hung Englishmen in Florida. Mr. Cleveland's great claim upon the gratitude of his countrymen has been the fearless resolution with which he has cancelled the legislative work of representative bodies, whether as Mayor, Governor, or President.

This function has become the more important in proportion as politics have been abandoned by the better conducted and the industrious portion of the people, and handed over to men who find their means of livelihood in organizing party meetings.

During the long ascendancy of the Virginia Dynasty— from Jefferson to Monroe—the two most notable events

* *Cleveland's Writings*, p. 14.

were the extension of the United States across the Mississippi, and the war of 1812 with England. The purchase of Louisiana, which was part of the first policy, was technically a violation of Democratic principle, as it was an exercise of central authority not provided for by the Constitution ; but this party has always been ready for a forward policy as regards populations who have not accepted the true Democratic gospel, whether they were Indians, or Spaniards, or Englishmen. During their tenure of power they gradually adopted some of the theories of their defunct opponents, and became advocates of protection with the view of developing national industries ; but this was only for a brief period, and since 1828 they have practically always denounced a high tariff as legislation in the interest of a class—a tax on the labourer for the benefit of the capitalist.

The Presidency of Quincy Adams—1825-1828—was a period of transition. Elected as a Democrat, he gradually drifted into collision with his own party, favouring the demands for public works to be carried out by the Central Government, and for the increase of the tariff in protection of the rising industries of New England.

The people who urged an extension of the Federal powers became again an organized party under the name of Whigs, whilst Jackson gave a new and formidable development to the principles of Jefferson.

The eight years' administration of this celebrated man marked a very great change in the history of the party and of the country. In the first place, the election of Jackson of Tennessee was the assertion of the power of the States beyond the Alleghanies—those new States

which have ever since played a conspicuous part in the
Union.   A great portion of his life had been spent in
pioneer work, and he was altogether in contrast with the
men who had hitherto conducted public affairs.   He had
an almost fanatical belief in his mission, as the elect of
the people, to protect the public against the politician
and the capitalist.   His sincerity of purpose and daunt-
less spirit gave him a popular influence, such as no one
since Washington had enjoyed.   In his war upon the
Bank of the United States, there can be no question that
he was applying logically the principles of the Democratic
party.   The perpetuation of this great institution at
Philadelphia was not consistent with the struggle against
centralization which Jefferson had preached.   He was
not, however, qualified by his training to find a suitable
substitute for the system which he abolished ; and the
confusion which followed, and the violence of his
demeanour, have exposed him to the comments of Republican writers ; but he remains a very distinguished
example of the working of the one-man power, and is
entitled to rank as the second founder of the Democratic
party.

From Jackson's first assumption of office, in 1829,
until General Taylor's election, the Democrats had, with
the exception of a few months, twenty years more of
supremacy, and they returned to office in 1853, after the
Taylor-Fillmore term, for eight years more.   Out of the
seventy-two years which elapsed between the commencement of the first Presidency of Washington, and the
inauguration of Lincoln, the Democrats held office for
fifty-three years.   They may thus claim to have had the

control of the most important part of the work in the moulding of the American nation.

The Republicans, on the other hand, boast that their predecessors were the creators of that nation. It was the Federalists who overcame local jealousies and suspicions, tempered the niggardliness of the Northern agriculturists, soothed the pride of the Southern planters, and founded the Union. The traditions of New England, hard and narrow perhaps, but teeming with intellectual life and the spirit of organization, were largely theirs; whilst their commercial experience gave them the advantage in matters of finance and political construction. Their love of independence had generated the idea of a new people; their love of order in later years made the incidents of a state of slavery within the Republic intolerable to their habits of patient industry, discordant to the uniformity of their lives—and they poured out their blood and spent their treasure in a resolute effort to eradicate it for ever. Whilst their utterances are frequently marked by inflated sentiment, and their party organization has quite as often reeked of corruption as that of their rivals, they have generally in the Eastern cities included the great number of the well-to-do classes—the people who, in a new country, are naturally the most likely to possess intellectual activity.

They may fairly claim to represent the national idea, whilst the Democrats represent the national spirit.

Starting with the principle of universal equality, Democrats argue from it strictly that there may be as much political wisdom in a village of log-huts as in the palaces of Fifth Avenue, or the stately mansions of Western Boston. They were the champions of the pioneer. As the supporters of local rights, they became the natural allies of the slave-holding States in the earlier stages of the struggle made by those communities to continue their peculiar institution. They cherish the memory of the part they played in the wars against England, whilst in the great cities they establish connections among the poorer classes — neglected, or oppressed, or disliked by the wealthy. They thus secure relations with the European immigrant, and join hands with the Roman Catholics, rather than with those Protestant organizations which are still active throughout the Eastern States.

In one of the few distinctly party speeches delivered by Mr. Cleveland, when addressing the Democratic Club of New York, after the Republicans had returned to power, he said of his party:

"It insists upon that equality before the law which concedes the care and protection of the Government to simple manhood and citizenship. . . . Though heresy may sometimes have crept into its organization, and though party conduct may at times have been influenced by the shiftiness which is the habitual device of its opponents, there has always remained, deeply imbedded in its nature and character, that spirit of true Americanism, and that love of popular rights, which has made it indestructible in disaster and defeat."*

After most of this volume was written appeared the memoirs of Senator Sherman, a typical Republican. He describes the Republicans as "the party of national

* *Cleveland's Writings and Speeches,* 1892, pp. 247, 248.

policies." "The Democratic party," he says, "has a very popular name. It means a government through the people. But the Republican party has a still more popular name. It is a government by the Representatives of the people." Delegation, however, and not representation, is the fundamental idea of the Declaration of Independence, and in this point of view, Democratic teaching comes nearer to the original theory of the Republic.

The Whigs, who became a party under Quincy Adams, exhausted their strength in various devices to rally the Northern States in favour of a stronger central system, whilst they sought to avoid collision with the slave-holding interest. After two attempts to secure power, they finally made way for the modern Republicans, who represented the current opinion of the Northern States that, irrespective of State rights, slavery must be got rid of in the South, as thoroughly as it had been got rid of, some sixty years before, in the North.

The Democratic party met them on the same lines which had marked their struggle with the old Whigs. They, like Henry Clay and Webster, were neither for nor against slavery, but they were against any aggression by the central power on the States; and when, in fear of this aggression, the Southern States took up arms, the old Democratic party was, for the time, completely shattered to pieces. The Democrats of the West and of the North vied with the Republicans in carrying on the war. Not only had they lost a large portion of their voting strength in the Union by the secession of the South, but their special theories of local liberty and limitation of central authority were discredited for a generation. Half the Cabinet of Lincoln were Democrats. Local chiefs were present on many a bloody field, asserting in person the national power against local opinion.

Two or three times after the termination of the war, they secured a majority in the House of Representatives. In 1876 their organization had so far recovered that they all but succeeded in winning a Presidential election; but it was not until twenty-four years after the retirement of Buchanan that the Democrats once again sent a representative to the White House in the person of Grover Cleveland.

If we enquire into the actual composition of the two parties at the present date, it will be found that the Democrats consist of the planters, a large portion of the agricultural classes, and the labourers; whilst the Republicans include the manufacturers and the large capitalists. The one party boasts greater numbers and more authority in the country districts; the other in the great commercial cities of the East and the North West.*

A reference to the manifestoes issued by each party after the war shows that the main burden of the Republican story was the necessity for securing the working of those amendments to the Constitution which had been passed in the interests of the coloured population, and for maintaining the principle of national unity against impenitent rebellion. Much stress was

* Mr. Tilden, the Democratic candidate of 1876, described the Republican party as those who live by the use of their wits, and the Democrats as those who live by the use of their hands.

laid on the duty of protecting American industry against the foreign importer.

The Democrats, on the other hand, when opposing Grant's re-election in 1872, urged a more speedy restoration of local government in the South, and advocated Civil Service Reform. In 1876 they denounced the delay in returning to specie payments, and the extravagance of administration, again demanded Civil Service Reform, and a reduction of the tariff. The unpopularity of General Grant's second administration gave them a great opportunity. Although they failed to make Mr. Tilden President, they secured majorities in both Houses of Congress, and the veto power of the President became as popular with the Republicans as it has since been among the supporters of Mr. Cleveland. In 1880 the Democrats continued their protest in favour of local rights, and formally adopted the phrase, "a tariff for revenue only"; whilst the supporters of Mr. Garfield contended that the tariff should be so adjusted as to favour American labour. Civil Service Reform was in fact a cry common to both sides. Neither party had very clear views on currency, whilst on tariff the line was distinctly marked—the Democrats contending that no money should be levied which was not required for the cost of government—the Republicans, that high duties kept up the rate of wages, and fostered the industrial progress of the Union.

It was in this condition of political affairs that Mr. Cleveland consented to be proposed to the National Convention held at Chicago in July, 1884, as the Democratic candidate for the Presidency.

The choice of a President is a long business, which may be divided into two acts. There is, first, the nomination of a candidate by each party. For this purpose, delegates assemble from all the local organisations, in what is called a National Convention; but which, in the eye of the law, is only a private meeting of citizens holding certain opinions. When each party has made its choice, the second act begins—the canvass of the country preliminary to the polling in November.

NOTE TO CHAPTER IV.

DECLARATION OF INDEPENDENCE, JULY 4TH, 1776.

"When, in the course of human events, it becomes necessary for one people to dissolve the political bands which have connected them with another, and to assume, among the powers of the earth, the separate and equal station to which the laws of nature and of nature's God entitle them, a decent respect to the opinions of mankind requires that they should declare the causes which impel them to the separation.

"We hold these truths to be self-evident : that all men are created equal ; that they are endowed by their Creator with certain unalienable rights ; that among these are life, liberty, and the pursuit of happiness. That to secure these rights, governments are instituted among men, deriving their just powers from the consent of the governed; that whenever any form of government becomes destructive of these ends, it is the right of the people to alter or to abolish it, and to institute new government, laying its foundation on such principles, and organizing its powers in such form, as to them shall seem most likely to effect their safety and happiness. Prudence, indeed, will dictate that governments long established should not be changed for light and transient causes ; and accordingly all experience hath shown that mankind are more disposed to suffer, while evils are sufferable, than to right themselves by abolishing the forms to which they are accustomed. But when a long train of abuses and usurpations, pursuing invariably the same object, evinces a design to reduce them under absolute despotism, it is their right, it is their duty, to throw off such government, and to provide new guards for their future security. Such has been the patient sufferance of these colonies; and such is now the necessity which constrains them to alter their former systems of government. The history of the present King of Great Britain is a history of repeated injuries and usurpations, all having in direct object the establishment of an absolute tyranny over these States. To prove this, let facts be submitted to a candid world.

" He has refused his assent to laws the most wholesome and necessary to the public good."

Then follow twenty-six other charges against King George.

CHAPTER V.

CONTEST FOR THE PRESIDENCY.

Position of the Republicans—J. G. Blaine—Reform movement—
Hostility of professional politicians to Cleveland—The Mugwumps
—The Tariff—The memories of the Civil War—" Rum, Romanism,
and Rebellion "—Large majority for Cleveland.

IN the Presidential contest of 1884, the Republicans
had some initial disadvantages to contend against.
The nation desired a change. It was tired of the self-
glorification of the Republican party, and attributed the
general corruption to their monoply of power during
twenty-four years. The scandals of the second Grant
Administration had been notorious, and under Mr.
Arthur's Presidency the Star Route enquiry, and similar
disclosures, showed what little progress had been made
towards that regeneration of political life which the public
fondly hoped for on the installation of General Garfield.
In such circumstances the proposal to give Mr. Arthur a
second term found little support, and the party hesitated
between Senator Sherman, of Ohio, and Mr. J. G. Blaine,
who, after General Grant, was the most conspicuous
figure in the Republican camp.

He had been Secretary of State to President Garfield ;
but the imputation of abusing his position as Speaker of

the **House of** Representatives, by levying contributions
from a railway company, persistently clung to him, and
his nomination by the National Convention at Chicago
alienated **at** once those active members of the party who
had been striving to purify the political atmosphere. **He**
could boast, no doubt, of abilities far above the average ;
nevertheless he was odious, apart altogether from the
Little Rock scandals, **to every sincere** patriot, **as a** man
who, through **a long career, prostituted his** great talents
by encouraging **every popular** delusion. **A** zealous
admirer thus **described him: "A live** man always abreast
of the times, he never **allows** himself **to** fall behind **a**
single **step." To** be first in the favour **of the** crowd was
the object he pursued all through life.

The Democrats, on **the** other **hand, both in New** York
and Pennsylvania, had **taken an active part in the uprising**
against professional politicians. **In the contest between
Hayes and Tilden the country** thought **that party had**
been **unfairly treated, and had given a good** example of
admirable self-control **and** thorough loyalty **to the Con-**
stitution. There **were** many independent men, **too, who**
desired the return **of** the Democrats to **power, as** marking
the final conclusion of **the war period.**

The special **feature of the political** situation in 1884
was the culmination of that movement for Reform in local
government, which **had** been **proceeding for some years**
past. **This was not the monopoly of one party or** another :
it was the outcome of general **discontent at the prevalence
of abuses in public** administration ; **and vast numbers of**
people were ready **to vote** with the **Democrats, not from**
any **clear preference for** their political **creed, so** much as

because they were the party opposed to the men who had so long held office. The sentiment in favour of something better than the existing condition of political life took the positive form of a separate organization to promote the success of the Democratic nominee. 'Mugwump' was the popular name applied by professional politicians to those who had become indifferent to the behests of the local leaders. A Mugwump has been defined as a person who never goes to the poll except to vote against someone. In 1884 they went, not so much to vote against Blaine, as to vote for Cleveland.

Among the Democrats this Reform movement was led by the County Democracy, which has been already mentioned as an organization distinct from the City committee,—familiarly known as Tammany. This was the body which had, in 1882, selected Cleveland as the candidate of the party, for the Governorship of the State.

The Democratic Convention was held at Chicago a month later than that of the Republicans, and it was determined to choose a candidate who, in personal character and political independence, should be in marked contrast with Mr. Blaine. Mr. Cleveland had the great advantage over distinguished competitors like Mr. Bayard, Mr. Thurman, and Mr. Carlisle, that he had never made his appearance in the political circus. Although a staunch Democrat, he had been twice called to important offices by the independent support of both parties. He was the very antithesis of the professional politician. His nomination was strongly opposed by this class among the New York Delegation; but their hostility was overborne, and he was nominated on the second ballot.* He was at once promised the support of distinguished Republicans like George William Curtis, Carl Schurz, Henry Ward Beecher, whilst the independent press throughout the States east of the Mississippi warmly espoused his cause.

There was nothing very new in the Democratic platform of 1884. The principal topics were the inexpediency of continuing political power in the hands of one party, and the importance of limiting taxation to the requirements of the State.

The first resolution was, "No taxes, direct or indirect, can be rightfully imposed upon the people except to meet the expenses of an economically administered government."

When Mr. Cleveland received from the Convention the formal announcement of his nomination, he replied in the following letter, which is his first recorded statement of party policy : †

"Your formal announcement does not, of course, convey to me the first information of the result of the Convention lately held by the Democracy of the nation : and yet when, as I listen to your message, I see about me representatives from all parts of the land of the great party, which, claiming to be the party of the people, asks them to entrust to it the administration of their government, and when I consider, under the influence of the

* A majority at a National Convention, whether it be a simple majority as among the Republicans, or a two-thirds majority as among the Democrats, is measured by the whole number of Delegates sent ; and where there are several candidates the balloting may go on for some days.

† *Writings and Speeches of Grover Cleveland*, p. 8, by GEORGE F. PARKER, New York. Cassell Publishing Co., 1892.

stern reality which the present surroundings create, that I have been chosen to represent the plans, purposes, and the policy of the Democratic party, I am profoundly impressed by the solemnity of the occasion, and by the responsibility of my position.

"Though I gratefully appreciate it, I do not at this moment congratulate myself upon the distinguished honor which has been conferred upon me, because my mind is full of an anxious desire to perform well the part which has been assigned to me. Nor do I at this moment forget that the rights and interests of more than fifty millions of my fellow-citizens are involved in our efforts to gain Democratic supremacy. . . . We go forth not merely to obtain a partisan advantage, but pledged to give to those who trust us the utmost benefit of a pure and honest administration of national affairs."

Neither in Mr. Cleveland's letters of acceptance, nor in the two speeches he made during the contest—one in New Jersey, and the other in Connecticut—did he take any partisan line.

The Republican declaration of policy recounted the achievements of the party since 1860, and asserted that duties should be levied on foreign imports "not for revenue only," but such as "to afford security to our diversified industries, and protection to the rights and wages of the labourer."

Mr. Blaine exerted to the utmost his natural energy and considerable gifts of language in order to justify the choice of his party. In a series of vigorous speeches delivered in various States, he boldly claimed all the progress of the country since the time of Lincoln as the result of high tariff, and drew appalling pictures of what might ensue if "the men who organized the Rebellion' were allowed "to seize the Government of the Union."

In his letter accepting nomination, he said :

"Almost the first act of the Republicans, when they came into power in 1861, was the establishment of the principle of Protection to American labour and American capital. This principle the Republican party has ever since steadily maintained ; whilst, on the other hand, the Democratic party in Congress has persistently warred upon it. Twice within that period our opponents have destroyed tariffs arranged for protection ; and since the close of the Civil War, whenever they have controlled the House of Representatives, hostile legislation has been attempted."*

He made liberal professions in favour of Civil Service Reform, advocated "a standard that shall enable the Republic to use the silver from its mines, as an auxiliary to gold, in settling the balances of commercial exchange."†

There is the following indication of the foreign policy which he subsequently developed when Secretary to President Harrison :

"With the nations of the Western Hemisphere we should cultivate closer relations ; and for our common prosperity and advancement we should invite them all to join with us in an agreement that for the future all international troubles in North or South America shall be adjusted by impartial arbitration, and not by arms."

An example of the way in which the tariff question was presented, is afforded by his speech in Brooklyn a few days before the poll :

"Certainly there is no man intelligent enough to reckon up his week's wages on Saturday night who does not know that the only difference between a day's pay for labour in the United States, and a day's pay for labour in the British Isles, is that which is produced by, and results

* *Blaine's Political Discussions*, p. 420. Norwich, 1887.
† *Ibid.* p. 433.

from, the Protective tariff; so that the American labourer
or mechanic who voluntarily casts his ballot for the
elevation to power of a party committed to Free Trade,
casts his ballot for the reduction of his own wages."*

The American people have justly claimed credit for the
total absence of rancour and vindictiveness which they
showed after the long struggle of the Civil War. This is
in truth a greater glory to both sections of the nation
than the splendid endurance, the tenacity of purpose,
and the brilliant military achievements which marked
that terrible contest. In spite of the influence of more
magnanimous feelings, it was not in human nature that
fierce memories should not smoulder on; and to the
hatred and wrath engendered by this conflict, Mr. Blaine
did not hesitate to appeal. Speaking at Fort Wayne, he
said:

"I do not believe that the men who added lustre
and renown to your State, through four years of brave
service in a bloody war, can be used to call to the
administration of the government the men who organized
the Rebellion."

The vote of the reconstructed Northern States, he
argued, must be all-powerful in the Democratic party.

"There is not one measure of banking, of tariff, of
finance, of public credit, of pensions, not one line of
administration on which the government is conducted
to-day, to which the Democrats of the South are not
recorded as hostile; and to give them control would
mean a change the like of which has not been known
in modern times. It would be as if the dead Stuarts
were restored to the throne of England; as if the
Bourbons should be invited to administer the govern-

---

* *Blaine's Political Discussions*, p. 460. Norwich, 1887.

ment of the French Republic; as if the Florentine Dukes should be called back and empowered to govern the new kingdom of Italy as consolidated by Victor Emmanuel.

* * * * *

"To call that section now to the rulership of the nation would disturb its own social and political economy, would rekindle smouldering passions; and under the peculiar leadership to which it would be subjected, it would organize an administration of resentment, of reprisal, of revenge." *

Again, at Terre Haute, speaking of the support given the Democrats in Indiana and New York, he said :

"Do the citizens of those two States fully comprehend what it means to trust the national credit, the national finances, the national pensions, the Protective system, and all the great interests which are under the control of the National Government, to the old South, with its bitterness, its unreconcilable temper, its narrowness of vision, its hostility to all Northern interests, its constant longing to revive an impossible past, its absolute incapacity to measure the sweep of the present and the magnitude of our future?" †

As the contest proceeded, Dr. Burchard stimulated the excitement by a denunciation of the poor relations of the Democratic party. The liquor interest in New York City, the Irish, and the South, were grouped together as "Rum, Romanism, and Rebellion."

Allusions to the Civil War were a common topic in the speeches even of the more responsible leaders of the party. Senator Sherman said to the Republicans of Washington :

"You have to meet the main forces and principles

* *Blaine's Political Discussions,* p. 448.   † *Ibid.* p. 451.

that opposed the Union army in war; that opposed the abolition of slavery; that sought to impair the public credit; that resisted a resumption of specie payment." *

These quotations are not made in order to convict the Republicans of "waving the bloody shirt," but to remind European readers how real the memories of the War still are for a great number of American politicians. Crowds of men who bore arms against each other in that struggle continue to meet, not on the field of battle, but in Congress. Of the present House of Representatives, nearly a third served in either Federal or Confederate armies. As late as 1892, Senator Sherman referred to the fact that whilst General Harrison had fought for the Union, Mr. Cleveland could boast no such claim to the confidence of his fellow-citizens. He declared that Mr. Cleveland was better than his party; but added there is this to be said of him, that "he was a man full grown at the opening of the War—an able-bodied man when the War was on. I have never known, nor has it ever been proved, that he had any heart for or sympathies with the Union soldier or the Union cause." †

The fairness of this observation may be judged from the following facts. When the war crisis came, Grover Cleveland was the only one of Fally Cleveland's nine children who was earning a fair salary, having secured $1000 a year. An elder brother, Richard Cecil, and a younger, Louis Frederick, were already serving under the Union flag; and it was considered that the con-

* *Sherman's Recollections*, p. 887.
† *Ibid.* p. 1171.

tinuance of his help for the widow and her children ought to be secured. Accordingly he borrowed money to obtain a substitute.

No stone was left unturned by the Republican agents; no invention was too mean to discredit their opponent. The fact that he was outside the regular political ring was relied upon as proof of his obscurity, whilst gross imputations were made against his private life. Mr. Cleveland met these attacks with a calm indifference, which has had a distinct effect upon Presidential contests ever since; and there is some reason to hope that the marked absence of personality in the contests of 1888 and 1892 may indicate a permanent improvement.*

When the polling was over, some question was raised as to the actual figures from New York; but it was soon ascertained that the Republican domination had at length been broken. Mr. Cleveland and Mr. Hendricks were elected respectively President and Vice-President by 219 votes against 182 for Blaine and Logan. Of the thirty-eight States then voting, twenty went to Cleveland, including New York, Connecticut, New Jersey, Delaware, Indiana, and Kentucky. For Blaine were Pennsylvania, the New England States, the North West and the trans-Mississippi States, except Texas.

---

* After the election, it became known that a person whom Mr. Cleveland had appointed to the Post-office at Copiah, Mass., had published a gross libel upon Mr. Blaine, and the President at once cancelled the appointment.

NOTE TO CHAPTER V.

The mode of electing the President is prescribed by the Constitution, and differs from the ordinary direct vote of a city for a Mayor, or of a State for a Governor. Each State chooses a number of electors equal to the number of Senators and of Representatives combined, which the State sends to Congress. The number of Senators is always fixed at two for each State. The number of Representatives varies with the population of the State. The mode of appointing the electors has varied since 1789. They are now chosen by a ballot of the whole State on the understanding that they do not exercise any opinion of their own, but simply vote for a particular candidate named to each voter at the time of their election. Thus the success of the list of either party in New York, for instance, means that thirty-six votes go to the Democratic or Republican candidate, as the case may be.

Under this system, the Presidential candidate appeals to the whole mass of electors throughout the Union, now numbering over twelve million ; but it is a consequence of the rule of double election that he may have a majority of the votes polled in the Union, and yet may lose the election because he has not a majority of the electors chosen by the States.

Mr. Cleveland, for instance, has always had a majority of voters since he first appeared as a Presidential candidate ; but he was defeated on the second occasion because small majorities within New York and Indiana gave both these States, or fifty-one "electoral" votes, to General Harrison.

If there is not an absolute majority of the electors in favour of any one of the candidates, the choice passes to the House of Representatives, who vote by States.

CHAPTER VI.

FIRST PRESIDENCY, 1885–86.

Inauguration—Choice of Cabinet—Reconciling influence—Visit to the South—First Message, December, 1885—State of Parties in 49th Congress—Resumption of public lands—Limited power of President—Vetoes—Pension Bills—Public buildings—The Texas Seed Bill—Wedding, June 22nd, 1886.

THE triumph of 1884 did not work any change in the character of Mr. Cleveland. At the White House, as at Buffalo and at Albany, he was the same unflinching champion of common sense and morality; but the faults of the legislative bodies are more inveterate at Washington; whilst the public, to whom the President appeals, is diffused over a much vaster area, and thus his capacity to secure the policy he aims at is less immediately operative. It is one of the peculiarities of American history, that in it date and number play a very important part. Anyone who has read the Constitution with some care, and fixed in his memory a few of the red-letter years of Republican history, such as the first election of Washington, has a convenient framework for his notes of the national story. Even death is not allowed to interfere with this Pythagorean order for more than a year or two. Tyler succeeds to Harrison, or Johnson to Lincoln,

Arthur to Garfield, without breaking the stated chronological sequence. The diligent arithmetician can count up Congresses as well as Presidents ; for the term of each Congress was fixed in 1787, and the power of dissolution is not known to the Constitution.

A still more remarkable result of this numerical arrangement is, that the transfer of power is necessarily attended with considerable delay. As it must take place at a time fixed long beforehand, irrespective of the actual condition of public business, it is, perhaps, essential that there should be a certain interval between the notice of dismissal given to one Administration, and the installation of another.

The elections for Congress and the higher public offices, including the President, take place in the November of the fourth year of office of the current term, but the citizen then elected does not become President until the 4th March following ; whilst the House of Representatives, which has been chosen on the same wave of opinion, is not generally called together until the December of the next year. Congress being only elected for two years, the President has, therefore, only the first and second years of his term of office in which his position as leader of the nation is assured him. It very rarely happens that the tide of public feeling at a Presidential election attains so high a mark in the Congressional pollings which occur in the middle of the Presidential term.

After Mr. Cleveland's election in November, 1884, he continued to rule the State of New York, from Albany, until January, when he resigned the office of Governor into the **hands of Mr. D. B.** Hill, the Deputy-Governor. **Meanwhile,** President Arthur and Mr. Frelinghuyzen carried **on** the government of the Republic **until March, 1885.** Then came the installation **of the new** President, of **whose** personal appearance **the reader** may here like to have some details, beyond **what the** portrait reproduced in this **volume** supplies When he entered on his great office **he had not** yet **completed** his 48th **year. Considerably above the** middle height, he does **not appear so tall as he really** is, having inherited, **perhaps** through his German grandmother, considerable **bulk of frame.** Dominating this massive figure **is a countenance** expressive of resolution **in every** trait. **It is eminently** the face of **a** man of action; **but** the **expanse of forehead,** and **the** penetrating, kindly glance, qualify **the impatience of the mouth and** the sternness **of** the brows.

On the 4th March, innumerable **crowds** attended **him** to the **Capitol,** where he **took the oath of** office prescribed **by the** Constitution. **From the front** of **the** Parliament **House he delivered the** address called **the** Inaugural, **which, in its way, is the most** interesting survival of Democratic **ideas. It is not prescribed by** the **Constitution, it has no** official recognition. **It is** the one **occasion** on which the President is supposed **to** speak to the nation at large in his own person. **Custom has deprived him of the opportunity of addressing either House of** Congress **by word of** mouth; **but on the 4th of March,** standing **on** the steps of the Capitol, **he, the first** citizen **of the Republic, speaks** to his **friends and fellow-** countrymen **for the last time** during **his period of office.**

This impressive function, in 1885, had special significance from the fact that it symbolized the conclusion of
the fierce conflict of a generation. From North to South
the conquerors and the conquered met again, under the
leadership of that political party on whom historic
connection with the South had entailed exclusion from
office for more than twenty years. Multitudes, who had
never journeyed so far north since the War, thronged
to Washington, not in any spirit of exultation, but in
order to realize for themselves this renewed assurance
of peace and equality for all citizens of the Republic.
According to the excellent practice—rarely departed
from—the ex-President, Mr. Arthur, attended the meeting, which lost none of its significance from the simple
dignity of Mr. Cleveland. He took advantage of his
professional experience as a speaker, to adopt a course
which the numerous political orators who had preceded
him in office perhaps thought beneath the dignity of
such occasions. Instead of a written address, he delivered a brief speech, in which he expressed his sense
of his great responsibilities, and his faith in a system
of "government by the people."

Space only allows of the following extracts:

"To-day the executive branch of the Government is
transferred to new keeping. But this is still the Government of all the people, and it should be none the less an
object of their affectionate solicitude. At this hour the
animosities of political strife, the bitterness of partisan
defeat, and the exultation of partisan triumph, should be
supplanted by an ungrudging acquiescence in the popular
will, and a sober, conscientious concern for the general
weal. Moreover, if from this hour we cheerfully and
honestly abandon all sectional prejudice and distrust, and

determine, with manly confidence in one another, to work out harmoniously the achievements of our national destiny, we shall deserve to realize all the benefits which our happy form of government can bestow. . . .

"In the discharge of my official duty I shall endeavour to be guided by a just and unrestrained construction of the Constitution, a careful observance of the distinction between the powers granted to the Federal Government and those reserved to the State or to the people, and by a cautious appreciation of those functions which, by the Constitution and laws, have been especially assigned to the executive branch of the Government.

"But he who takes the oath to-day to preserve, protect, and defend the Constitution of the United States, only assumes the solemn obligation which every patriotic citizen—on the farm, in the workshop, in the busy marts of trade, and everywhere—should share with him. The Constitution which prescribes his oath, my countrymen, is yours; the government you have chosen him to administer, for a time, is yours; the suffrage which executes the will of freemen is yours; the laws and the entire scheme of our civil rule, from the town meeting to the State capitals and the national capital, are yours. Your every voter, as surely as your Chief Magistrate under the same high sanction, though in a different sphere, exercises a public trust. Nor is this all. Every citizen owes to the country a vigilant watch and close scrutiny of its public servants, and a fair and reasonable estimate of their fidelity and usefulness. Thus is the people's will impressed upon the whole framework of our civil polity—municipal, State, and Federal; and this is the price of our liberty, and the inspiration of our faith in the Republic."

The next day public curiosity was relieved by the announcement of the names of the new Cabinet. In theory these officers, seven in number, are, with one exception—that of Secretary to the Treasury—the clerical staff of the President. They are selected by him, and may be removed by him without any cause assigned, although their appointment needs confirmation from the Senate. To a new President this is given as a matter of course. Although the Independents had afforded Mr. Cleveland substantial support—not perhaps more votes than he lost from the distrust of the professional politicians —it was understood that they did not expect any place in his Cabinet. What the country desired was to test the question, how far the Democratic party were capable of carrying on the government under the reconstructed Union. Men wanted assurance that there was a second party in the State to whom they could look for competent administration. They desired, too, that the South should feel at home in the new system which had come into being since the War. Accordingly there was neither surprise nor disappointment when it was found that all the members of the new Cabinet were Democrats. Public opinion had already designated Mr. Bayard, of Delaware, as Secretary of State or Chief of the Cabinet. His name had been mentioned more than once as a candidate for the Presidential chair. A man of high character, he represented the older elements of the party who, in a hopeless minority, had fought many stiff battles against the "carpet baggers," and against public extravagance. The Secretaryship of the Interior was given to Mr. Lamar, Senator of Mississippi, a distinguished lawyer who has since proved a valuable addition to the bench of the Supreme Court. The party in the North-West were recognized in the person of Mr. Vilas, of Wisconsin, who had presided over the National Convention, and who became Postmaster-General. Mr. Endicott, who had

been Judge of the Supreme Court in Massachusetts, was
named Secretary of War, and Mr. Garland, of Arkansas,
Attorney-General. The nominations of Mr. Manning to
the Treasury, and of Mr. W. C. Whitney to the Navy,
were objected to by rivals and by censorious critics as
savouring of favouritism, since both these Ministers came
from the President's own State, New York. They both,
however, reflected lustre on the Administration. The
United States Navy had been altogether neglected after
the War, until the days of President Arthur, when some
steps were taken for reorganizing it in a manner be-
fitting the extent of American commerce. This work
Mr. Whitney took up with vigour, and the great position
which the American Navy now holds is very much due to
the activity and resource of this Minister. The condition
of financial affairs made Mr. Manning's post the most
important in the Cabinet, and his reports during the two
years he held office, before failing health obliged him to
retire, showed a complete mastery of fiscal and economic
problems.

The progress made in the noble work of reconcilia-
tion which Mr. Cleveland was elected to carry on, was
signalized at the national demonstration on the death of
General Grant. In his first year of office it became his
duty to announce to the country the decease of the great
Republican soldier, and in the proclamation he issued on
that occasion he condoled with his fellow-citizens on the
loss of "a great military leader who was, in the hour of
victory, magnanimous ; amidst disaster, serene and self-
sustained. The great heart of the nation, that followed
him when living with love and pride, bows now in sorrow

above him dead, tenderly mindful of his virtues and his great patriotic services."

It has been already mentioned that the inauguration in March had brought to Washington visitors from many Southern States whose inhabitants, except such as came as members of Congress, had not been seen in the capital for nearly a generation. The funeral of Grant was marked by a still more striking proof of the new era. Numbers of the surviving officers of the Confederate army attended to do honour to the victor of the North. Among the pall bearers were Confederate generals, and the most distinguished of the mourners was the first Democratic President since the War.

The following year he made a formal visit, accompanied by the principal members of his Cabinet, to the State Fair at Richmond, the chief city of Virginia, and formerly the capital of the Confederate Congress.

After dwelling on the glories of Virginia, "the old Dominion State," the mother of Presidents, he went on to point out that one of the great functions of a State was the contribution it made towards the training of American citizens.

"It must be the same wherever seen, and its quality is neither sound nor genuine unless it grows to deck and beautify an entire and united nation, nor unless it supports and sustains the institutions and the government founded to protect American liberty and happiness. . . . .

"If in the past we have been estranged, and the cultivation of American citizenship has been interrupted, your enthusiastic welcome of to-day demonstrates that there is an end to such estrangement, and that the time of suspicion and fear is succeeded by an era of faith and confidence."

The restoration of the Democratic party to public life and the general work of administration proceeded happily, but the outlook on the side of Congress was not equally cheerful. To men whose political experience is limited to the English parliamentary system, the powers given to the President under the Constitution look enormous; closer examination shows, however, that they are for the most part negative rather than positive. The Constitution, with the securities which the veto provided against immature schemes of legislation, seemed to its framers in 1787 sufficient for all practical purposes, but the relations of man to man have attained much greater complexity with the development of national wealth and the extension of territory. The population of the Union is now 60,000,000 people * instead of 2,500,000 in 1780, and its area some 3,000,000 square miles instead of 356,445.

The President can veto any bills, however important; he has a multitude of small posts to fill on his own responsibility; but in appointing to all the higher offices— the seats in the Cabinet, vacancies in the Supreme Court, Foreign Embassies,—he in his turn is exposed to a veto by the Senate. In his dealings with foreign Governments he has hardly an even share of power with the Foreign Affairs Committee of the Senate. If legislation is required, he is authorized by the Constitution to recommend to the consideration of Congress any measures which he shall judge necessary or expedient; but for defending these recommen-

* The actual population is now, I believe, larger, but these figures are taken for convenience as an average during the period covered. In 1885 Mr. Manning estimated the population at fifty-two millions.

dations in the House he is dependent on such assistance as chance may put in his way. Poor as is the debating power of these assemblies, they enjoy a direct share in the work of administration by means of standing committees. Over fifty of these bodies are appointed by the Speaker of the House of Representatives in each Congress, and it is in conference with them that the heads of departments settle the details of the various bills which the President may suggest in his message.

The condition of the currency which resulted from the expedients adopted during the War, and from the varying policy of subsequent Congresses, constituted a grave and constant danger. Another evil was that, owing to the maintenance of the high duties required to meet the expenses of the Civil War, the Treasury received large quantities of money for which it had no proper use, and these funds remained stored up in the Government coffers instead of supplying, as they naturally should, the ordinary channels of circulation.

In the forty-ninth Congress, which met in December, 1885, the Democrats boasted a majority of forty in the House of Representatives ; but of the Senate the majority was Republican. In his first annual message, the President, after reviewing the relations of the Union to foreign countries, invoked the aid of Congress to obtain a settlement of the controversy with Great Britain concerning the North American Fisheries, and proposed the appointment of a Commission for this purpose. He then proceeded to advocate a reduction of import duties, in a passage which emphasizes a fact forgotten by European critics, namely, that the Democratic party are not free traders within the meaning of that term as understood by the followers of Mr. Cobden. With Free Trade in the abstract they have no concern. Their contention is of a simpler kind, that the Treasury ought not to receive more money than its expenditure makes necessary.

"The fact that our revenues are in excess of the actual needs of an economical administration of the government, justifies a reduction in the amount exacted from the people for its support. Our Government is but the means established by the will of a free people, by which certain principles are applied which they have adopted for their benefit and protection; and it is never better administered, and its true spirit is never better observed, than when the people's taxation for its support is scrupulously limited to the actual necessity of expenditure, and distributed according to a just and equitable plan.

"The proposition with which we have to deal is the reduction of the revenue received by the Government, and indirectly paid by the people from Customs duties. The question of Free Trade is not involved, nor is there now any occasion for the general discussion of the wisdom or expediency of a Protective system.

"Justice and fairness dictate that in any modification of our present laws relating to revenue, the industries which have been encouraged by such laws, and in which our citizens have large investments, should not be ruthlessly injured or destroyed. We should also deal with the subject in such a manner as to protect the interests of American labour, which is the capital of our working men; its stability and proper remuneration furnish the most justifiable pretext for a Protective policy.

"The Treasury," he continued, "is placed in a false position, by being compelled under the Bland Act to spend every year $24,000,000 in purchasing silver to be coined into dollars which no one will use."

Another important topic dealt with in this message was the recovery of portions of the public domains, which, granted by the Government for the common benefit of the United States, have been appropriated to individuals, and thus "the policy of many homes" has been sacrificed to that of large estates.*

On this latter subject considerable progress was subsequently made, not by the help of Congress, but in spite of violent opposition from members of that body. The great railway companies had obtained grants of land along their lines, but instead of letting them in small allotments to settlers, preferred leasing them to large speculators, or to grazing or farming companies. The Land Department, however, proceeded to examine into cases of this kind; many grants were revoked, the lands brought again within the disposition of the Department, and made available for persons willing to settle on them. It was the boast of the Democratic party in 1888 that through these exertions 100,000,000 acres of the public domain had been recovered from corporations and syndicates, and restored to the people to be used for homesteads.†

This achievement may serve to remind us of facts which are frequently lost sight of by admirers of American institutions. The reports of the Land Office show that during the last ten years there have been allotted annually, on the average, over 6,000,000 homesteads; that is to say, homes have been found each year for a population

---

* President's Message, 8th December, 1885, p. 37.

† Mr. George F. Parker states that if account is taken of the notices running against unlawful occupation of the public domain when the President left office, the total number of acres recovered is nearly 146,000,000 acres. (*Life of Cleveland*, p. 193. 1892.)

many times larger than that of London. The vast resources of this kind within the control of the Government have, perhaps, more to do with the prosperous working of the American Constitution than that public opinion to which Mr. Bryce attributes such healing qualities. However that may be, there can be little doubt that when all these unoccupied lands have been taken up, a new chapter of American history will be opened.

The President's success in recovering the public domain from the railway companies was possible, because the law was clear, and the officials set in motion by him were able to carry it out; but on questions which required the aid of legislation, it was in vain that he asked for any assistance from Congress. Over and over again he repeated his argument for the repeal of the Bland Act, which compelled him to buy silver and coin it into dollars which the public would not use.*

Although his efforts to secure the abolition of improvident laws were fruitless, the veto enabled him to put some curb on fresh projects of extravagance.

The fact that the Treasury surplus was increasing at the rate of many millions sterling a year, was a serious anxiety to the classes who were interested in maintaining a high rate of taxation on imports; and their representatives bestirred themselves to find some means of employing a portion at least of this vast hoard. Any proposal

---

* It was only on his return to office in 1893, when the storm he had repeatedly foretold actually broke over the nation, that he succeeded in repealing the Act which compelled the Treasury to purchase silver. (See p. 164.)

for spending money was welcomed, whether the object proposed was a handsome post-office in some remote locality, or a pension to some soldier or his widow.

There was already in operation a liberal scheme of pensions for the survivors of the War who had suffered any physical injury, and for those supported by them. A special department was charged to look after the administration of the funds allocated by Congress. It was argued, however, that there were many exceptional cases of hardship which did not come within the rules of the Pension Commission and the general act which that body administered ; that a wealthy, generous nation ought to make liberal provision for soldiers who had suffered in the struggle for national unity. The practice was introduced of passing special acts to grant pensions, or increase those already granted, to invalids who had served in the War, or to the relatives dependent on them. This expenditure had been increasing for some time, and the forty-ninth Congress was bent on encouraging it. A great business of pension agency sprang up, and bills were brought in by the hundred. Mr. Cleveland then had recourse to the authority exercised with such effect at Buffalo and at Albany. To the great indignation of "the soldiers' friends," the veto was used without stint or hesitation. All the cases for which these bills were passed had, it must be remembered, been submitted in the first instance to the Pension Bureau. When a bill came up for his approval, the President obtained a report from that body, and then proceeded to examine the application and the evidence himself. Such a practice added immensely to his labours ; but he was not a man to shrink from toil when a vicious system of this kind challenged exposure.

The theory of the law was that the pension had been earned by injuries sustained whilst on service. In one case a pension was claimed by a mother because her son, when on furlough, had died of the small-pox; another sturdy applicant was a man who, when away from his regiment on leave, had received a blow on the head in a dispute at a drinking bar. Medical evidence of permanent injury was, in many of these claims, of the most flimsy description.

A report from a Committee of Congress expresses with some pathos the chagrin felt at the President's interference with the generosity of the people's representatives.

"So extraordinary is the censure, sometimes rudely expressed, and in nearly every instance severely implied, of the action of the two Houses of Congress and of their Committees, upon whom has devolved the wearisome and generally unappreciated labour of investigating these claims, accompanied, in many cases, by such ridicule of, and evident disgust with, the claims themselves, that your Committee feel that they are justified in a brief review of the circumstances involved.*

" In doing this, a strong effort will be made to restrain a not unnatural feeling of indignation. Much criticism has been indulged in by the President of the methods of legislation pursued by the two Houses of Congress; and, however uninformed he may be upon the subject, and however unintentionally, by reason of want of knowledge, he may have misrepresented to the country the methods of legislation which have been pursued in like cases ever since Congresses and Parliaments have existed, and which have, since Parliaments became free, been safe from Kingly and Presidential interference; all the same the

* *Congressional Record*, vol. 17, p. 7780.

G

people are misled by the unwarranted statements of the President as to the manner in which legislation upon previous claims, and the like, is, and of necessity must be, conducted."

During his first Presidency, Mr. Cleveland used the veto power three hundred and seven times. Nearly three hundred of these bills were grants of pension; and only in one case of pension was the rejected measure subsequently passed by the requisite two-thirds majority of both Houses, and in that instance it was agreed that the Pension Bureau, on whose report the President had acted, had been misinformed.*

Most of the other vetoes of President Cleveland were upon grants for Federal buildings. The President insisted that the first question in such cases was whether the building was required for the despatch of public business.

"The care and protection which the Government owes to the people do not embrace the grant of public buildings to decorate thriving and prosperous cities and villages, nor should such buildings be erected upon any theory of fair distribution among localities. The Government is not an almoner of gifts among the people, but an instrumentality by which the people's affairs should be conducted on business principles, regulated by the public needs."

The Texas Seed Bill was open to a similar objection of principle. A run of bad weather had produced considerable agricultural distress in this State, and it was proposed to make a grant of public money, which was to be spent in supplying seed to the farmers.

* The appropriation for pensions was $80,000,000 in 1880. In 1891, the third year of the Harrison administration, it had risen to $146,000,000.

The President took advantage of the occasion to warn
the country against the system of appealing to the Government for gifts.

"I can find no warrant for such an appropriation
in the Constitution, and I do not believe that the
power and duty of the general Government ought to
be extended to the relief of individual suffering which
is in no manner properly related to the public service
or benefit. A prevalent tendency to disregard the
limited mission of this power and duty should, I think,
be steadfastly resisted to the end; that the lesson should
be constantly enforced that, though the people support
the Government, the Government should not support
the people." *

This declaration, that there was no reciprocity in
the payment of public money between the people and
the Government, supplied a convenient text to those
who endeavoured to resist the extravagance of the next
Administration.

In 1886 occurred an interesting event, upon which,
when discussing the career of a living statesman, I
should hesitate to enlarge, were it not that the considerable space assigned to it by American writers illustrates
a special characteristic of political life in the Republic.
The publicity given to every detail concerning the personal
career of men engaged in the business of the nation,
is one of the tributes which opinion rigorously exacts;
and not to give some account of the wedding at the
White House, would be to ignore the habits of the
people over whom Mr. Cleveland has so long presided.

Mr. Hensel thus introduces the subject of the President's marriage:

* *Cleveland's Writings,* p. 450.

" While there has never been any tendency in the United States to imitate the Court customs of European countries, interest has always been strong in the domestic life of our public men, and especially of those called to the Presidency.

" While the majority have been drawn from the average plain life of the plain people of the country, our history does not present a single case in which the men elected President, or who succeeded as Vice-Presidents, were not of gentlemanly social aspect, and their families, if they had them, did not do the honour of the White House with credit to themselves and their country." *

There had been many widowers in occupation of the White House; but the last Democratic President before the Civil War, Mr. Buchanan, and the first Democratic President after the War, Mr. Cleveland, are the only instances of Presidents who had not been hallowed by matrimony. At the commencement of the term, Mr. Cleveland depended on his youngest sister, Miss Rose Cleveland, to preside over the social functions connected with the President's position He was very much in the same position as Mr. Arthur, who, a widower, had had the assistance of his sister, Mrs. McElroy. Miss Cleveland shared the intellectual gifts of her family, and before undertaking these ceremonial duties, had pursued a successful career as a teacher.

It gradually became known that notwithstanding the cares of silver and tariff, and the worrying applications of importunate office-seekers, the President had thoughts for other things, and might one day become a bridegroom. Washington society rapidly came to the conclusion

* HENSEL'S *Cleveland,* p. 180.

that the lady of the President's choice had not been found in that city, and curiosity was very eager to ascertain who she might be. The secret, however, was carefully kept, and it was only a few weeks before the 2nd June that the engagement with Miss Frances Folsom became publicly known.

This young lady was the daughter of Mr. Oscar Folsom, who has been already mentioned as one of Mr. Cleveland's associates in the profession of the law. A young man of generous temperament and great abilities, he was a partner in the firm of Vanderpoel and Laning, but had been killed in an accident, shortly after his friend Cleveland, on the expiration of his term of office as Sheriff of Erie county, had joined the firm subsequently known as Cleveland and Bissel. His daughter was born in Buffalo, in July, 1864, and under the supervision of her mother spent some years at the central school in that city. Her docility and mental power attracted the sympathy and admiration of her teachers. From the central school she passed on to Wells College; and it was here that the flowers sent her from the Governor's garden at Albany first set the friends of the maiden student dreaming of the possible future in store for her. These speculations became more active as each success of the intellectual girl was marked by fresh tributes, no longer from Albany, but from Washington. In June, 1885, she completed with distinction her graduate course, and went to reside for some months in a neighbouring county of New York, with her grandfather, Colonel John B. Folsom, of Folsomdale. As autumn came round she started with her mother for a tour in Europe, a course of travel which was prolonged until she arrived at New York, on the 27th May in the following year, to receive the greetings of her future sister-in-law, Miss Cleveland.

The good taste of the two families had hitherto baffled the indefatigable activity of the American pressman, but now he was to be indulged with a wedding at the White House. There had been many marryings at this historic mansion before, but they had been of the sons and grandsons, or the daughters and granddaughters of Presidents or their friends. This was the first occasion on which the Chief Magistrate of the Union celebrated his wedding during his term of office. For the decorations of the Blue Room, of the Green Parlour and the East Parlour, and for the dresses of the company who attended the ceremony at seven o'clock in the evening of the 2nd June, I must refer my readers to the newspapers of the day, or to Mr. Hensel. In deference to Republican theory there was no State ceremonial The Diplomatic Corps were not invited, the guests including only the Cabinet and the immediate friends of both families.

The honeymoon was brief; and on June 15th, the tall graceful girl, who was not yet twenty, entered upon her important duties as the colleague of the President in social functions. In spite of Jeffersonian theories, Washington has become one of the great society centres of the world; and it is no intrusion into the private life of the President to say that the gracious bearing and feminine tact of his youthful spouse have largely contributed to spread that respect for, and sympathy with, the personality of the President, which have extended his political influence throughout the Union.

The masses of his fellow citizens, always inclined to treat reserve as a sign of exclusiveness, savouring of aristocracy and other European vices, were much disposed to claim the President's wife as a sort of national property; and even when he was out of office, the birth of his daughter Ethel in 1891 was celebrated all over the country as an augury of triumph for the Democratic party at the next election. " Baby Cleveland " was almost as popular a cry at the election of 1892 as " Tippecanoe " had been in the days of General Taylor, and " Forty four, forty, or fight," in the canvass of President Polk.

Whilst Mr. Cleveland, however, submitted to these expressions of cordiality from "a plain people," he discouraged the tendency to connect personal rank with the members of the President's household. Towards the end of his first administration, Mrs. Cleveland was asked to preside over a popular ceremonial which the President was unable to attend owing to the state of public business, and the invitation was declined on the ground that the President's wife could not discharge any public function apart from her husband. She was his helpmate at the White House and his companion at many social gatherings; but, unless accompanied by the President, she had no public precedence over any other lady who might attend the proposed celebration.

CHAPTER VII.

THE TARIFF MESSAGE, 1887.

Mercantilism and Democracy—Slavery—Silver—Protective Duties—
Democrats favourable to Protection on National Grounds—From
1820 Advocates of Reduced Tariff—The "Tariff of Abominations"
—The "Compromise" Tariff—Return to Protection on Lincoln's
Election—High Duties during the War—Reduction of Debt—
Enormous Surpluses—Cleveland's Attack on the Tariff System.

THE first great work of Mr. Cleveland in higher
politics was the recall of the Democratic party to
a full share of activity in public life. The second was
the revival of their struggle against high tariff. Since
the War, they had not distinctly resumed their position
on this question until Mr. Cleveland brought it to the
front in 1887.

Whilst the last session of the forty-ninth Congress
dragged on, the President made up his mind to promulgate a distinct policy at the opening of the next Congress
in December, 1887. There was no more probability
of loyal co-operation from that body than from the
preceding one. The second Congress of the quadrennial
term is generally occupied in observation of the chances
of the Presidential election which occurs in the November
between its first and second session. The first session

is a kind of tournament, sometimes prolonged through the whole eleven months, each party or section of a party seeking to win popular favour by sallies in one direction or another. Mr. Cleveland determined to take advantage of this spirit of enterprise, in order to revive the old policy of the Democratic party, the reduction of duties. The election for this fiftieth Congress had shown a great decline in party strength. The Democratic majority in the House of Representatives was reduced by nearly one half, whilst the Republicans still retained command of the Senate. But if legislation was impossible, the formal demand for it might focus public attention on one at least of the two great objects for which he had in vain asked the help of the previous Congress.

Casting aside the old practice, which makes the annual message a digest of the State papers of the year, he devoted the whole of the message of December, 1887, to an appeal for a reduction of tariff.

This document will probably remain the most famous of Mr. Cleveland's State papers; but before examining it in detail, it is necessary to glance at the previous history of tariff legislation. The English controversies about Protection and Free Trade bear only in a very remote degree upon the questions of tariff policy which have divided American parties since 1820. In order to understand the significance of the struggle against high duties, we must keep in mind the nature of their government and the trading instinct of the inhabitants. With a young nation engaged in the pursuits of industry, the predominance given to popular influence by their institutions has made their political system peculiarly sensitive to the material wants and to the financial enterprises of the inhabitants. To provide opportunities of making money came to be considered the true object of government. Hence economic questions supply the key to the history of the Union during the greater part of this century.

Dislike of the aristocratic influences prevailing in the old world plunged them into revolution in 1776. A passion for national existence, a resolution to escape the fissiparous tendency conspicuous in the Spanish Republics, produced the Civil War of eighty years later. If we except these periods of moral elation, when the spirit of the people rose to a higher plane, the whole preoccupation of Americans has been economic expansion. The bringing into cultivation the vast domain of the West, the gradual substitution of manufacturing industry for agriculture in the East, the development of cotton planting, the great mining activity which set in after their dominion reached the Rocky Mountains— these have been the immediate concerns of the people. The adaptation of all these opportunities to what Mr. Andrew White calls "mercantilism,"* has been the main employment of American statesmen during the whole of the present century. Although at the time of the revolution their industry was agricultural rather than manufacturing, they were, from the first, a nation of merchants. Their farm produce was not for home consumption merely, but for export. The exchange through the West Indies of agricultural products for

* *Message of the Nineteenth Century to the Twentieth.* By A. D. WHITE. Newhaven, 1883.

European manufactures, the export of corn to Europe, the shipbuilding in New England—these pursuits gave them early training in commerce, together with a spirit of adventure and keen scent for money returns.

The conception of the future of the Republic, cherished alike by Washington and Jefferson, was that of an agricultural people in undisturbed enjoyment of rural prosperity, free from the excitement and the vices of great trading cities. This ideal seemed adapted to the existing facts of American life. It was congenial to that passion for exalting country life, in contrast with the town, which Rousseau had made popular. Even before the close of the century the increasing power of the great cities of the North was a subject of apprehension to Jefferson. The establishment of Congress in the sylvan seclusion of the district of Columbia was desired, not so much from any fear of mob violence, as with the view of isolating the delegates of the people from the corrupting influence of wealthy combinations. But the spirit of speculation, of commercial enterprise, was alive in the country; and when a new discovery opened to the planter an unthought-of source of wealth, this commercial impulse spread with marvellous rapidity over those Southern regions where the accumulations of the trading cities had been regarded with envy and distrust. Suddenly a despised product of the plantation, the cotton plant, gave a promise of fortune eclipsing altogether the profits on rice or tobacco.

Until towards the close of the last century, the English manufacturer mainly depended for his supplies of raw cotton on the West Indies, a small quantity only coming from islands off the coast of Carolina. The ordinary

American cotton, owing to the shortness of its staple, could not be worked with profit by the machinery then in use. The inventions of Arkwright and Crompton made the upland cotton available, but the expense of separating it from the pod imposed considerable limitations on its manufacture. Then came, in 1793, the cotton-gin of the American inventor, Eli Whitney.* The slave, whose labour hitherto had been only sufficient to prepare 1 lb. of cotton a day, was, with the cotton-gin, able to deal with 50 lbs. in the same time. Slavery had been quietly dying out of the land. Provision had been made by the Constitution for the abolition of the Slave Trade by 1808, and one State after another had followed the example of Massachusetts in arranging for the liberation of all slaves within its borders. It was only in 1804 that slavery ceased in Rhode Island. Wherever cotton could be grown, this tendency was at once arrested by the new demand for cotton and labour to tend it. However well founded the theory, that the use of slave labour was not good economy, there was no time for working out these ideas, when every planter found in the supply of black muscle under his control a source of immediate wealth nearly as great as the mines of California or of Colorado in subsequent years. Not only was the extinction of slavery checked, not only was the slave household made available for work on the old plantations; a great system of slave-breeding was promptly established to meet the demand for labour on soil fit for growing cotton in the territories of the Mississippi valley. The principle of State rights acquired a new significance as a

* RHODES' *History of the United States*, vol. i. p. 26.

safeguard against the anti-slavery sentiment of the
North; and henceforth all the political appliances of
the States which retained slavery were directed to
defend their new opportunities of fortune, and secure
scope for extending their business in the great interior,
of which the aboriginal inhabitants were being gradually
exterminated or expelled. The production of cotton in
1791 was 2,000,000 lbs. for the whole of the United
States. In 1804 it had risen to 80,000,000 lbs. At once
all the expedients which the Constitution put at the
command of the voter were called into play to secure the
development of this new means of growing rich. A
slave-owning interest was organized at Washington, and
from the war of 1814, until 1860, the protection of the
slave-holder was the main occupation of Congress.

Under this influence the provisions of the Constitution
were wrenched, and nearly every leading man of both
parties, from Benton to Webster, was sooner or later
pressed into the service of the slave interest. Thus a
series of inventions which has contributed to the
prosperity, well-being, and social advancement of an
important part of the English people, which has done
more than any discovery of modern times to bring
decency and comfort to remote populations of the
earth, had upon the American nation, under a political
organization extremely sensitive to gusts of popular
appetite, the effect of checking social progress for two
generations, and finally plunging the country into the
most bloody civil war recorded in history.

There are many other instances of this susceptibility of
American government to some theory of an immediate

money advantage to the voter ; and it is this idiosyncrasy of the great Republic which renders the one-man power, created by the Constitution of 1787-8, so valuable and so popular. It is true that in monarchies and aristocracies political power has been used to promote the pecuniary interests of individuals and of classes ; but these systems of government have, in modern days at least, proceeded in certain grooves of custom, and never had, except in some era of civil war, the free scope which, were it not for the veto, a State Legislature or a Congress might command with a majority in both chambers belonging to one and the same party. In the American Republic, the passion of gain encounters no restraining influences of class or habit, and hasty cupidity wells through all the channels of their political organism.

What happened with regard to cotton planting recurred later on in the case of tariff, the railway interest, and the mining power of the Far West. Each combination in succession was able to appropriate for its own ends that political machinery which had been devised for the protection of the liberty and the property of individuals.

The Democrats were the instruments of this usurpation in regard to black labour. To save them from similar bondage to the owners of silver has been the purpose of Cleveland. The Republicans have now for nearly three generations been clay in the hands of the manufacturing interest. They have been used to levy taxes upon the agriculturist and the consuming masses, in order to ensure high profits to the mill-owner.

Whilst the slave interest was carrying all before it in the South and West, the North had undergone a

momentous change.   At the time of the Revolution,
most textile fabrics in use were homespun.   With the
development of the factory system in England, the proportion of imported goods became larger every year, and
the trade in agricultural produce was encouraged by the
European wars.*

As the struggle in Europe became fiercer, the Berlin
and Milan decrees of Napoleon, and the English Orders
in Council, stopped the accustomed channels of commercial exchange.   Disputes about neutral rights highly
inflamed the public mind, and Jefferson had recourse to
the expedient of the Embargo.   Then came the Non-
Intercourse Act of 1809, and ultimately the war of 1812.
Commerce with England was prohibited, and at an end.
There was at this time a sudden growth of factories for
the production of cotton goods, woollen, and iron and
other manufactured articles, which had previously been
obtained from England.   By 1815, manufacturing industry
had taken firm root in the country.   Then, with the
peace of Ghent, came a flood of English goods; and
although the shipping interest of the North, which had
suffered severely during the War, contended for Free
Trade, there arose from the factory centres a loud cry for
Protection.   Appeal was made to the example of the
great nations of Europe, who recognized import duties as
a part of public policy.   Hamilton had, in his report on
manufactures, as early as 1792, urged, with great power,
the patriotic duty of making the Republic independent of
the foreigner.   The Tariff Act of 1816 was a recognition

---

* In 1803 there were only four cotton mills in the entire Union.
TAUSSIG, *Tariff History of the United States*, p. 27.

of the principle of Protection, the levying of duties for
the benefit of the home producer; but this was more
apparent in the arguments used in support of the Government by the youthful orators of the time, like Clay, than
in the provisions of the Act itself. Calhoun supported
it on the ground that certain industries ought to be made
national, such as cordage used in navigation.

The interest of the tariff question in these earlier years
is that the Democratic Republicans were favourable to
Protectionist legislation, partly from national jealousy of
the foreigner, partly from a desire that the Government of
their party should have ample funds to pay off the debts
contracted during the War.

Meanwhile increased use of machinery in England
made the supply of European goods cheaper and cheaper;
and with the advent of peace in Europe, there was a
steady falling off in the demand for the agricultural
produce of the States. The theory of securing a home
market for struggling industries gained strength until
the Act of 1828, the "Tariff of Abominations," which
finally cured the Democratic Republicans of their senti-
mental interest in Protection. Webster, as the brilliant
gladiator of New England, had, in view of the shipping
interest, at first opposed import duties. But as manufacturing enterprise grew stronger his policy changed, and in
later years he found himself competing with Clay as the
advocate of a system of high tariff. Democrats contended
that whilst Protection was necessary in order to prevent
the collapse of industries called into existence for the
supply of national wants during the War, and was useful
to secure the permanent establishment within the territory

of certain other industries essential to national defence, taxation, subject to these considerations, should be limited to the needs of the Government.

The era of prosperity which set in after 1819 had removed any apprehension as to want of revenue to pay off the National Debt; but against any proposal to reduce the tariff, the Whigs pleaded the importance of public works. For the establishment of great lines of communication, such as the Cumberland Road, the States had not adequate resources in capital or legislative jurisdiction. The question of Internal Improvements became for some years the dividing line in politics. As the successors of the Federalist party, the Whigs clamoured for expenditure on roads, harbours, and canals, which should bring the different States into closer relations with each other, and render the territories of the West accessible from the Eastern ports. Madison vetoed the proposal for making the Cumberland Road at the expense of the nation. As a rule the Democrats consistently resisted the policy of Internal Improvements, alleging that it tended to increase the power of the Central Government over the States, led to waste, encouraged speculation, and served as an excuse for unnecessary taxation.*

In 1828, as at the present day, much diversity of opinion existed as to what home products should be protected. Whilst the Whigs differed in each locality as to the subjects of taxation, the Democrats could not agree on the principle of Protection. The supporters

---

* See Mr. Cleveland's Veto of the River and Harbour Bill, May 29, 1896, p. 231.

of General Jackson in the South were opposed to high duties, but his following in the Northern States clamoured for Protection to manufactured goods. Each party tried to make the bill then before Congress so offensive to some other section as to ensure its rejection by them; but no section would take the responsibility of defeating it, and the result was that a general scheme of Protection slipped through, so odious to everyone, that a reaction was inevitable. Then came a long struggle, until in 1833 Henry Clay carried the Compromise Tariff, which saved his clients from any considerable reduction of duties at the time, but on condition that, gradually, all duties should reach a general level of 20 per cent. From that date onwards the fall in duties continued, with a brief reaction during the Taylor Presidency, until the election of 1860 brought the Republicans into power.

It is commonly assumed that the present tariff system is the result of the Civil War, but before the Civil War began, the Republicans had unfurled the flag of Protection. The Morill Tariff Bill passed the House of Representatives in the session preceding the election of Lincoln. It was a bid for the support of the manufacturing interest, although it did not become law until the following year. Its professed object was to substitute duties levied on certain articles or quantities, and called "specific duties," for those levied on the value of the goods, and called *ad valorem.*

There are some plausible arguments against *ad valorem* duties, but the Protectionist hostility to them arose from the fact that the consumer was able to see more clearly

than he could in a system of specific duties, the amount
of the burden which Congress imposed upon him.
These changes in the mode of levying duties have
generally been made a pretext for a considerable addition in the duties paid. Accordingly, by this act of
1861, the rates on iron and on wool were substantially
increased. High duties practically form an indispensable
part of Republican policy.

Afterwards, with the need of the Treasury to provide
funds for raising armies, came the Internal Revenue
Act of 1864, imposing heavy taxes upon every article of
consumption. The Government, it is estimated, received
between eight and fifteen per cent. on every finished
product. It was naturally contended that duties should
be imposed to balance the internal taxation, to put
domestic producers in the same situation, so far as foreign
competition was concerned, as if the internal taxes had
not been raised. Here was the opportunity for the
advocates of Protection. The majority of the men
who had so long opposed high duties were in the
Confederate camp. Among the Northern constituencies,
money to carry on the war was the one consideration,
and there prevailed "a furor of taxation," of which the
Morill Tariff Act of 1864 was the outcome. Every
domestic producer who asked for a duty against his
foreign competitor had his claim assented to: Protection
ran riot; and this, moreover, not merely for the time
being. Not only during the war, but for several years
after it, all feeling of opposition to high import duties
almost entirely disappeared.

On the conclusion of the war, the reduction of internal

taxes was immediately taken in hand, but no corresponding change was made in import duties. On the contrary, there was in many cases an actual increase, although the two original arguments for the revival of Protection, namely, the high internal taxation and the enormous war expenditure, had ceased to exist. By 1872 all the new internal taxes on home industry had been abolished. Taxes on spirits and beer, on banks, and a few smaller imposts, such as that on patent medicines, were all that remained of the duties on home produce.

Just as the Embargo of Jefferson and the war of 1812 created a manufacturing interest, the high tariff of the Civil War gave an enormous development to home manufacture of all kinds. In 1872 the claimants for Protection were more numerous and powerful than they had been in 1860, whilst the old party of low duties was struggling for bare existence. The enormous debt supplied a strong argument for maintaining a large public revenue, and such changes as were made in the tariff were directed to render it more consistent and complete as a system of Protection.

There was a considerable demand from the Western States for reduction of taxation in 1872, and this was met with great adroitness by Mr. Blaine and his friends. Revenue duties, such as those on tea and coffee, were completely swept away, whilst the manufacturers claimed credit for a general reduction of 10 per cent. on all other dutiable articles. When, after the commercial difficulties of 1873, there was a renewal of apprehension as to the state of the revenue and the means for meeting the public burdens, the duties on articles which competed with home productions were again raised, and the protected interests recovered the ground they had temporarily yielded.   In the case of wool and woollen stuffs, Professor Taussig instances various ingenious alterations in the mode of assessment, whereby the duty was, after the War, considerably increased.   The Copper Act, 1869, is a striking example of Protectionist enterprise.   Up to that year the duty on ore was 5 per cent., whilst on bars and ingots it was two and a-half cents per pound, and copper industries sprang up in Boston and Baltimore.   Upon the discovery of the rich mines on the southern shore of Lake Superior, the price of this metal fell, and the representatives of Wisconsin and Michigan obtained from Congress an increase to 25 per cent. in place of 5 per cent. on ore, and ingot copper was to pay five cents per pound instead of two and a-half cents.   This act destroyed the smelting establishments on the coast, which had obtained ore from Chili and other places abroad, and it made it possible for the copper producers at home to enter into a combination to keep up the price of their produce.

There are not only the local and personal interests connected with the particular trade to be considered; there are the local and personal interests of other members of Congress, whose help may be secured, or whose opposition may be neutralized. *

* Of the Woollens Act of 1867 and the Copper Act of 1869, Professor Taussig says: "The details of these acts, and of other acts passed since the war, have undoubtedly been settled in large part by men who had a direct pecuniary interest in securing an increase of the duties." (TAUSSIG, *Tariff History*, 1894, p. 228.)

It is on the veto power that the public have hitherto relied, as some security against the tendency of each member of Congress to look at all schemes of policy with the view of ascertaining how many dollars his friends, or his locality, or his State are likely to make out of the proposal.

To gauge the rival principles of Free Trade and Protection, would be obviously beyond the range of this little volume. The Tariff Acts in America are chiefly remarkable as examples of the readiness with which their political system succumbs to the pressure of private interests, and of the extreme susceptibility to current ideas of personal advantage. This is the tendency which Mr. Cleveland has combated through his whole career by his free use of the veto in earlier years, and subsequently, by his labours as a national leader, to secure the repeal of the Sherman and the McKinley Acts. By resolute opposition to legislative intrigue, by the frankness of his utterances as a public man, Cleveland, ever since he entered public life, has made it his aim to restore the political institutions of his country to their proper functions, and prevent them from being used merely for money getting.

In 1883, towards the close of President Arthur's administration, the continuance of large annual surpluses excited attention, and a Commission was appointed to propose lower duties. A conference of the two Houses resulted in a bill which made nominal reductions on a variety of articles, nearly all of which were the produce of home industry; whilst in the case of many kinds of goods in which an important import trade existed, considerable additions were made to the rates charged.

In 1884 Mr. Morrison, a Democrat from Illinois, appealed to a Democratic Chamber to reduce the tariff, and asked for a reduction of 20 per cent. on all duties.   His bill was rejected by five votes ; but in the majority of 150 there were forty-one Democrats, coming principally from States where the parties were evenly balanced, such as Pennsylvania, Ohio, and New York. Accordingly, although the Democratic party declared for revision of the tariff in 1884, they endeavoured to conciliate protected interests.   They demanded that, in levying customs, all materials used in arts and manu-factures and the necessaries of life, not produced in the Union, should be free, and that, when customs duties were imposed, the law should be carefully adjusted to promote American enterprise.   It was a question, the party managers felt, which could not be approached without a certain amount of caution.   Protection of the protected had been the main theme of Mr. Blaine's letter of acceptance, and of most of his subsequent speeches ;* but Mr. Cleveland directed his arguments to show that every taxpayer was entitled to demand an economic use of the moneys taken from him.   Speaking in New Jersey, he said : "The right of the Government to exact tribute from the citizen is limited to its actual necessities, and every cent taken from the people beyond that required for their protection by the Government is no better than robbery." †

* See chapter v. p. 61.
† *Cleveland's Writings*, p. 301.

In the inaugural address he maintained that the people should be relieved from unnecessary taxation, and that there should not be an accumulation in the Treasury, "a temptation to extravagance and waste."

In his first annual message he returned to the subject of revenue. The Treasury had a surplus of $70,000,000.

"The question of Free Trade is not involved, nor is there now any occasion for the general discussion of the wisdom or expediency of a Protective system.

"Justness and fairness dictate that in any modification of our present laws relating to revenue, the industries and interests which have been encouraged by such laws, and in which our citizens have large investments, should not be ruthlessly injured or destroyed. We should also deal with the subject in such a manner as to protect the interests of American labour, which is the capital of our working men. Its stability and proper remuneration furnish the most justifiable pretext for a Protective policy.

"Within these limitations a certain reduction should be made in our customs revenue," and he went on to suggest that taxes upon imported necessaries should be repealed.

The language used by Mr. Cleveland did not indicate much confidence in the success of his recommendations, notwithstanding the Democratic victory in the previous year, and the fact of a substantial majority in the House of Representatives. In the Senate the Republicans still had a majority; but the difficulty of securing legislation did not arise so much from the strength of the Republicans as from the Protectionist element in the Democratic ranks. During the session Mr. Morrison, who still represented Illinois, returned to the subject, and introduced a bill making detailed changes in the tariff, which it was estimated would result in a reduction of

$20,000,000. This bill, like that of 1882, was met by an obstructive motion and defeated, 35 Democrats combining with 122 Republicans against the mass of the Democratic party. Of these 35, 23 came from the States of New York, Ohio, and Pennsylvania,* and it was apparent that nothing could be hoped for in the 49th Congress. In 1886 there was a further surplus of over $30,000,000, which, added to previous accumulations, made an excess over expenditure of close upon $94,000,000. The President urged reduction of duties on the opening of the winter session. A variety of arguments were stated against the continuance of such a system, but this appeal was ineffectual. No attempt at legislation on the subject was made that session.

It was in this state of affairs that on the opening of the 50th Congress in December, 1887, when the air was already filling with the sounds of preparation for the Presidential election of 1888, Mr. Cleveland made reduction of tariff the one topic of his message.

This discourse did not excite much hope that good would come of the new Congress. The message, it was felt, was addressed to the country at large in view of the coming election, and produced almost as much dismay among the wire-pullers of his own party as in the ranks of the Protectionists. The former apprehended loss of votes in the Eastern States. As "practical" men, they shook their heads and declared it very imprudent. Some of them even doubted if it were constitutional. It was all very well for a President to veto bills and to express pious opinions, but to attempt to get particular legislation carried

* *Quarterly Journal of Economics*, ii. pp. 69, 70.

through was dictating to Congress. The message, however, recalled the Democrats to the old principle of the
party, taxation for the purpose of revenue only. A tariff
reduction bill was carried through the House of
Representatives, with only four Democrats voting in the
minority; but in the Senate, where the Republicans still
had a majority, a bill was introduced changing the tariff
in the direction of increased protection. Both schemes
were intended as declarations of policy in view of the
coming election. The manufacturing interests, after
their first astonishment was over, immediately applied
all their resources to the organization of the electoral
campaign.

The general public received the message with enthusiasm.
The confidence which they had felt in the President as a
leader three years before was at once revived. Many of
his independent supporters had been disappointed at the
result of their demonstration in 1884. With Mr. Cleveland personally they had no fault to find, except that he
had not carried Civil Service Reform as far as they
expected; but in office he was necessarily thrown into
close relations with his own party, and the elder politicians did not appear in the least edified by the high
moral principles which had been talked about in 1884.
Once again, however, the President had shown that he
had opinions of his own, and meant to use his position
in public life in order to advance them. The struggle
thus opened was far too serious to make it a safe
means of securing a further term at the White House.
Whether he was to be elected again in 1888, or even
nominated, Mr. Cleveland felt confident that at the

corrupt system of levying taxes for the benefit of particular interests he had been able to strike a blow from which it must suffer for many a day.

When the election ended in the return of the Republicans to power, the practical people were still better satisfied with themselves and their political maxims; but the Protectionists, who had won the election, knew that the fight was not over. They were forced to go further, and rushed into the ambitious scheme of Mr. McKinley, in their endeavour to give some appearance of symmetry and logical strength to their system.

CHAPTER VIII.

A CAMPAIGN YEAR.

Preparation for the next Presidential Election—Tariff bills—Fishery debates—History of question—Treaties of 1783 and 1818—Reciprocity Treaty, 1854—Fishery Clauses of Treaty of Washington abrogated by President Arthur—Seizure of American vessels, 1886—Retaliation Act passed, 1887—The Chamberlain Mission—Treaty of 1888 sent to Senate—Senator Dolph on England—Treaty rejected by three votes—President asks additional powers of retaliation—Protocol adopted.

ONE curious effect of the American Constitution is, that the statesman chosen to carry out the national will finds only two years out of the four of his term available for practical legislation. During the latter half of the Presidency, politicians are absorbed in the preparations for the next election. Whether the incumbent of the White House be a candidate or not, the pre-occupation of all minds is the choice of a new Executive in the coming November. When that has been decided, there remains another session before the party which has been successful assumes the responsibilities of office.

The proceedings of the Fiftieth Congress, however, deserve some notice. The Democrats were defeated in 1888, and they had to wait until 1892 before there was any chance of carrying out the policy which their leader announced in December, 1887; but it was to the principles which Mr. Cleveland proclaimed in 1887 and 1888, and to his steadfast maintenance of these principles in defeat, that his supporters owed their return to power in 1892. The immediate result of the Tariff message was a display of unity such as the Democrats had not shown since their accession to office. In the House of Representatives only four members of the party voted against the bill introduced by Mr. Mills for the reduction of duties. He proposed to abolish the duties on hemp, flax, wool, and other raw materials, whilst those on manufactured and partly manufactured goods were reduced. Instead of accepting this moderate scheme, the Senate adopted the Allison Bill for increasing several of the more important taxes, such as those on fine cottons and woollens. Neither of these proposals was expected to pass. They were gages of battle, but the old traditional sentiment of the Democrats against Protection had been successfully appealed to, and the tariff became the question for the next Presidential election.

A great part of this session was devoted to the fishery disputes. Mr. Cleveland persevered in his attempts to arrive at some settlement, and the Senate seized the opportunity to discredit his policy.

Of all the controversies which have arisen between the United States and Great Britain, that concerning the rights of fishing off the coast of British America has been the most troublesome. When the independence of the Union was acknowledged in 1783, and the general principle of a boundary between the Union and the

provinces which remained under the dominion of the
English Crown was agreed upon, the fishing rights on
the coast of each territory became, by the law of nations,
appropriated to the respective inhabitants of the two
countries. Thus fishing off Newfoundland and the
coasts of the Dominion was under English authority,
all south of the boundary line belonged to the Union.
As a matter of fact, the fishing to the north has always
been infinitely more productive than that on the coast
of New England. The representatives of England who
assisted to frame the Treaty of Paris in 1783, were the
men who for some fifteen years had been denouncing
their own Government on account of its management
of American affairs. Their spirit of opposition had gone
so far as to exalt the founders of the Union to a position
in popular estimation which they retained for some
generations. Longing to be rid of an unfortunate
business, the new English Ministers were disposed to
make large concessions. Mr. Adams pertinaciously
asserted the claim of the States to a share in the whole
of the fishing which had fallen under British control after
the conquest of Canada, and by the third article of the
Treaty of Paris it was agreed that "the people of the
United States should continue to enjoy unmolested the
right to take fish of every kind on the Grand Bank, and
on all the other banks of Newfoundland; also in the
Gulf of St. Lawrence, and at all other places on the sea
where the inhabitants of both countries used at any time
heretofore to fish." Americans were also "to have liberty
to take fish of every kind on such part of the coast of
Newfoundland as British fishermen shall use," and also

"on the coasts, bays, and creeks of all other of His
Britannic Majesty's dominions in America." These concessions, however, did not include the right to dry or cure
fish on any of the settled parts of the British dominions.
It was only unsettled bays or creeks that could be used
for those purposes. By the subsequent Treaty of 1794,
a reciprocal and perfect liberty of commerce and
navigation was established between the two nations,
and the restrictions of the Treaty of 1783 fell into
abeyance.

Then came the war with England in 1812-14. When
negotiations for peace were opened in the winter of 1814,
the English envoys to Ghent declared that the concessions
made as regards the fisheries by the Treaty of 1783 had
been cancelled by the war, and they declined to revive
them unless some equivalent concessions were made to
British industry by the United States. After further conferences, it was finally arranged by the Treaty of 1818,
that the Americans should share with the British the
rights of deep sea fishing off Newfoundland and the
coast of Labrador, subject, however, to the former restriction against using any unsettled bay or creek for
curing or drying of fish. By a further clause the United
States renounced for ever any claim they had previously
made or enjoyed to fish within three marine miles of the
coasts, bays, or harbours not included in the preceding
clause. American fishermen, however, "shall be admitted
to enter such bays and harbours for the purpose of shelter
and repairing of damages, of purchasing wood and of
obtaining water, and for no other purpose whatever"; and
provision was made for the adoption of such rules as

might be necessary to guard against any abuse of this latter privilege.

The three miles limit was always interpreted as running seaward from the most advanced headland; thus very large bays were included in the waters specially reserved to Canada, and the practical effect was that from most of the inner waters south of Cape Ray in Newfoundland the American fisherman was shut out. This construction excluded him from fishing in bays, to some of which the entrance was fifty miles wide, and deprived him of access to the whole of the seaports under British dominion south of the St. Lawrence.

In all this region, along which the most remunerative portion of the fishing industry was carried on, Americans had no right to transgress the three mile limit except for the specified purposes—shelter from storm, repairs, purchase of wood, or taking in water. These were liberties which the ordinary considerations of humanity demanded. Two practical questions arose under this clause. There was plenty of fish outside the three mile limit, but the industry was carried on under great disadvantage when there was no access to the shore for the purpose of clearing the catch and having it cured on land. The skipper from Gloucester or Portland had, after a successful run, to spend precious time sailing south to the coast of New England in order to clear out his capture, and by the time he returned to the fishery ground the shoal had disappeared, and the golden opportunity was lost. An important consideration for deep sea fishing was the securing of an abundant supply of bait, and it could readily be had on the coast; but this was not one of the purposes for which the American fisherman was entitled to approach the shore.

The practical hardships of such a state of things were obvious; but the Canadian fishermen replied that they were merely a consequence of that difference of opinion which had produced a separation among the old British colonies. The men adjacent to the fisheries preferred to maintain their allegiance to the English crown : the New Englanders adopted another political arrangement. As to the question of hardship, there need be none if the Americans were willing to act reasonably. If they wished to participate in one of the natural advantages which the separation of the Colonies had left to the Canadians, let them give some benefit of similar value to Canadian industry.

The logic of this argument has never been directly disputed. Agreements were made from time to time by which, in consideration of the admission of fish and fish-oil to American markets, the New England fishermen were secured the rights which they had enjoyed, in common with Canadians, whilst they were all under the same sovereign.

The most remarkable of these friendly compacts was the Reciprocity Treaty of 1854. This permitted Americans to take all kinds of sea fish in the creeks and bays of British America, and also to use the shore for the purpose of drying nets and curing the catch. It secured the Canadians similar opportunities on the sea-coasts of the United States, and, what was more important, the admission of fish and other enumerated articles from Canada to the parts of the United States free of duty.

As the Protectionist party gained strength in the Republic, the terms of these various arrangements were criticized, and every now and then an existing treaty was denounced as giving unfair advantages to the Canadians. The Treaty of 1854 was abrogated by the Union in 1866, and both nations returned to the position they had occupied under the Treaty of 1818. There arose immediately an outcry against the Dominion for excluding the American fishermen from privileges for which the Union had refused to pay the stipulated price.

In the mind of the American masses, the leading ideas are the size and wealth of their community. Another is a confident belief that their political system is infinitely superior to any other. To people so disposed, the national rights of the British community on their northern border is a disagreeable accident, of which they are inclined to resent the inconvenience. Their foreign ministers cannot deny the title of the Canadians, but whenever the agreements, made on the principle of mutual concession, are brought to a termination, angry disputes instantly occur as to the application of the Canadian harbour rules, as to their reasonableness, or the authority of the local governments to issue them. Members of Congress are eloquent upon the iniquity of depriving American fishermen of facilities which they have enjoyed for years past, neglecting, however, the consideration that these conveniences had been previously obtained under compacts which the Union refused to keep up. The discontent became the greater, because as years went by, and the New

England towns increased rapidly in population, these localities constituted the most valuable market for the catch of the coastal waters, from which American fishing-boats were excluded. Railway communication, too, made these towns readily accessible to any fishermen who could clear their catch at Canadian ports. The principal provisions of the Reciprocity Treaty of 1854 were restored by the Fishery clauses of the Treaty of Washington in 1871. This document contained the important addition that a right of transit, free from duty, should be reciprocally secured to the Union and the Dominion in respect of ports of both countries, on the St. Lawrence, the lakes, and the adjoining rivers.

President Arthur, at the request of Congress, gave notice for the termination of this Treaty, and it was about to lapse on the 1st July, 1885, when Mr. Cleveland entered upon his first year of office, in March of that year. In order to avoid the contests and disputes likely to arise from the sudden interruption of fishing, which had been so long carried on under these reciprocity arrangements, it was proposed by England that if no new treaty had been signed when the period fixed by the notice of abrogation arrived, then the old system should be continued for the rest of the fishing season. Thus American fishermen were to be allowed the privileges conceded under the Treaty of 1871, six months after that treaty had lapsed by the action of their own Government, and the public would be saved from the inconvenience arising from the displacement of trade, and a sudden change in the area open for fishing purposes to American and Canadian fishermen respectively. Accordingly, in June, 1885, an agreement was made at Washington, extending the existing Fishery Treaty, which was to expire on July 1st, until the 31st December, so as to give time for a new treaty, and avoid the injury to individuals likely to result from a sudden return to the Treaty of 1818. The President on his part undertook to seek the aid of Congress with a view to a new treaty. This agreement had, as Congress was not in session, all the force of a treaty without the assent of the Senate. In his annual message in December following, after describing this temporary arrangement, he continued :

"Following out the intimation given by me when the extensory arrangement above described was negotiated, I recommend that Congress provide for the appointment of a Commission, in which the Governments of the United States and Great Britain shall be respectively represented, charged with the consideration, upon a just, equitable, and honourable basis, of the entire question of the fishing rights of the two Governments and their respective citizens, on the coasts of the United States and British North America."

So far from responding to the President's appeal, the Republican party seized the opportunity to denounce all such arrangements as snares for the American fishermen. Senator Frye declared that the fishery clauses of the Washington Treaty had been most disadvantageous to the Union ; and the Senate, by thirty-five votes to ten, resolved that the Commission "ought not to be provided by Congress." No intimation was given what course the President should take. This was for him and his advisers to determine ; but Congress would give him no assistance beyond such aid in putting pressure upon England as a general denunciation of all compromises might supply.

No agreement had been made when the fishery season opened. Canada had been deprived since January of the privileges she enjoyed under the fishery clauses of the Treaty of Washington; and still American fishermen proceeded to fish in Canadian waters, as in previous years. The result was a series of collisions between the fishermen and the Canadian authorities. One vessel after another was seized for fishing or attempting to fish in waters from which Americans were excluded by the Treaty of 1818.

Mr. Bayard, then Secretary of State, wrote a series of despatches, which afford an interesting example of the American style of argument. He did not deny or admit that the Treaty of 1818 was against him, but dwelt at length on the supposed grievances which it entailed in the altered conditions of the fishing trade. He urged that the language of the treaty had ceased to have any rational meaning; that the vessels seized might have been engaged in ordinary mercantile transactions, and therefore were not liable to seizure; that the interpretation of any treaty should be made by the Home Government, and not by the Dominion authorities.

This latter clause of the American case was in curious contrast with the complaint made by former diplomatists at Washington—that these questions were dealt with in London, instead of being left for settlement between the States and their neighbours in Canada. In the interval the federation of the Canadian provinces had given a new status to the Canadian people. They were much more likely to have opinions of their own in 1885 than in the days of President Polk.

In the autumn of 1886 Mr. Blaine made a violent attack on the President, alleging that the temporary renewal of the old fishery treaty the previous year was a defiance of the authority of the Congress, and an attempt to play into the hands of England.*

In March, 1887, Congress took up the subject from the Republican point of view, and passed a Retaliation Act, authorizing the President, whenever he was satisfied that American vessels had been denied entry to ports in British America, or had been unjustly vexed or harassed, to exclude vessels of the Dominion from all or any ports in the United States; also to exclude fish or other products of the Dominion.

The President, however, persevered in his efforts to effect a settlement. Mr. Chamberlain, Lord Sackville, and Sir Charles Tupper were appointed by England plenipotentiaries, to consider and adjust the existing controversies as to rights of fishery. The President named Messrs. Bayard, W. L. Putnam, and James Angell to act on behalf of the United States. In the autumn of 1887 these gentlemen met at Washington; and, after protracted deliberations, a treaty was agreed to on the 15th February, 1888.

Under this compact, the bays and creeks in which the United States agreed, by the Treaty of 1818, to renounce all rights of fishing, were divided into two classes. As regards a certain number of these waters,

* BLAINE's *Political Discussions,* p. 493.

a definite line of exclusion was specified in each case by article iv. The rest of the coastal waters were to be dealt with by four Commissioners, two for each country, who were to draw a line, not from headland to headland, as had hitherto been done by the Canadian authorities, but from any two projecting parts of the shore within the bay which came within ten miles of each other. Thus a large number of bays were opened to fishing, with no restriction beyond the three miles limit from the shore, except in the case of certain inner recesses, and for these the three miles limit was to be measured seawards from the ten miles line.

By another section, ships visiting the harbours for the special objects mentioned in the Treaty of 1818 were exempted from various liabilities as to pilotage, harbour dues, and so forth; and other concessions were made with the view of avoiding conflicts between the local authorities and American fishermen.

A very important article was number xv., which provided that in case both countries established reciprocity in regard to the duties on fish and fish-oil, annual licenses, free of charge, should be granted to American fishermen to enable them to use Canadian ports for a great variety of purposes, such as the purchase of bait and transhipment of catch.

When sending this agreement for adoption to the Senate, the President said :*

"I believe the treaty will be found to contain a just, honourable, and therefore satisfactory solution of the difficulties which have clouded our relations with our neighbours on our northern border. . . . .

* *Congressional Record*, vol. 19, p 1373, 21st Feb. 1888.

"The proposed delimitations of the lines of the exclusive fisheries from the common fisheries will give certainty and security as to the area of their legitimate field; the headland theory of imaginary lines is abandoned by Great Britain, and the specification in the treaty of certain named bays, especially provided for, gives satisfaction to the inhabitants of the shores without subtracting materially from the value or convenience of the fishery rights of Americans."

A scheme involving concessions on one side and the other was sure to be attacked, and, unfortunately, the American Constitution gives to political partisans a direct share in the treaty-making power. No arrangement made by the President with a foreign country has any validity until it has been ratified by the Senate. The President was held up to odium as an agent of England, and denounced, not only by Republican critics, but by mutineers of his own party. No light was thrown on the line of policy which might find acceptance with the Senate. To the argument that the leaving such a question unsettled might lead to international conflict, Mr. Dolph replied:

"Sir, our battles with Great Britain will be battles of diplomacy; she will get by diplomacy all that we are weak enough to yield; but the lessons taught her by experience have not been forgotten, and she will reserve the contest of arms for nations of less strength and fewer resources."*

After acrimonious debates, extending over three months, a decision was taken on August 21st, and ratification was refused by thirty votes to twenty-seven.

Two days after the rejection of the treaty the President sent a vigorous message asking for sweeping powers of

* *Congressional Record*, vol. 19, p. 6257.

retaliation against Canada, in case Canadian fishermen were interfered with.

The February treaty, he maintained, provided a satisfactory settlement ; but as the Senate had refused to sanction it, the next thing to be done was to take such measures as would prevent the Canadians from renewing their interference with American fishermen. Retaliation was the only course left open, and the retaliation, if entered upon, should be thorough and vigorous. The act of March he put aside as altogether inadequate, and pointed out that a further clause of the Washington Treaty had given Canadians the important right of transhipping goods from certain New England ports.

He asked for an act to enable him, " by proclamation, to suspend the operation of all laws and regulations permitting the transit of goods, wares, and merchandise, in bond, across or over the territory of the United States, to or from Canada." He further declared that the reciprocal rights of navigation on the Great Lakes, and the canals adjoining them, did not work fairly for American fishermen, and demanded additional powers with the view of securing equality.

This message was a surprise to the public, and seemed, at first sight, inconsistent with the sanction given to the treaty. It was, however, a natural consequence of the proceedings of the Senate. As Head of the State, it was his duty to make provision against the recurrence of disputes like those which had arisen in 1886. The simplest and best way of attaining this end was the treaty which Mr. Chamberlain and Mr. Bayard had agreed on. The factious spirit of the Senate, excited

by the approach of the Presidential election, had
destroyed that scheme, whilst the Republican party
endeavoured to divert attention from their proceedings
by general allegations that the President had not maintained a sufficiently firm attitude towards England. It
was important to make it clear, in view of possible
eventualities, that whatever he might think of the wisdom
or sense of fair play shown by his countrymen, he was
prepared to do everything in his power to protect their
individual interests.

The Senate made the message an occasion for further
invective. Senator Hoar denounced the President and
his advisers as "a dilatory and halting administration,"
declaring that if any legislation was required, it ought
to have been asked for long before. Senator Sherman
substituted for the consideration of the message a series
of resolutions, with the view of forcing upon Canada
a commercial union with the United States.

The plenipotentiaries had foreseen the possibility that
the Senate would refuse to confirm the treaty, and added
a protocol embodying a temporary arrangement by which
American fishing boats might, by taking out licenses at
an annual fee of 1\frac{1}{2}$ per ton, enjoy many of the privileges
which would have been secured to them under the treaty.
This proposal was adopted for two years, and is the basis
of the arrangement which has been continued to the
present day.

CHAPTER IX.

MR. CLEVELAND IN OPPOSITION.

Cleveland nominated by acclamation—His letter of acceptance—
General Harrison—Character of contest—Murchison incident—
Cleveland gets majority of votes, but not of electors—Concluding
session of Fiftieth Congress—Financial conditions of the Republic
—Veto of the Direct Tax Refunding Bill—Resumes work at the
Bar—Residence at New York—Buzzard's Bay—Political speeches
—Letter on silver—Popularity with the country.

AS the date for holding the National Conventions
drew near, the Democrats prepared confidently for
the struggle. This time the choice of a candidate was
not a matter of doubt.

In 1884 they had accepted Mr. Cleveland as the
nominee of New York reformers, rather than selected
him themselves. There was a prospect that with the aid
of the Independent vote, this great State might be carried,
and accordingly many veteran politicians better known to
newspaper readers, like Hendricks, Bayard, and Thurman,
were set aside. In 1888 the grumbling of the older
members of the party was suppressed, and all were convinced that in Cleveland they had a leader who enjoyed
a greater share of the confidence of the people than any
Democrat could boast for fifty years.

The Convention at St. Louis in June nominated him

by acclamation, an honour of which no one except General Grant had been the recipient since the second nomination of Jackson.

The declaration of party policy affirmed the principles of the anti-tariff message, and denounced unnecessary taxation. When the Committee of the Convention came to acquaint him with the result of their deliberation, he addressed to them a dissertation on the office of President and on the condition of public life, which is one of the most interesting of his public utterances. The passage setting out his theory of the National Executive has been already quoted.* He went on in striking terms to recount his experience of the great world of politics as he found it at Washington.

"Four years ago I knew that our chief Executive office, if not carefully guarded, might drift little by little away from the people to whom it belonged, and become a perversion of all that it ought to be; but I did not know how much its moorings had already been loosened.

"I knew four years ago how well devised were the principles of true Democracy for the successful operation of a government by the people and for the people; but I did not know how absolutely necessary their application then was for the restoration to the people of their safety and prosperity. I knew then that abuses and extravagances had crept into the management of public affairs; but I did not know their numerous forms, nor the tenacity of their grasp. I knew then something of the littleness of partisan obstruction; but I did not know how bitter, how reckless, and how shameless it could be."

Whilst the tariff message had rallied the Democratic party, it had produced something like dismay in the Republican ranks. Cleveland's "extraordinary message,"

* See page 45.

Senator Sherman calls it, with the natural amazement of a veteran Congressman who finds a politician actually grappling with a public question, instead of gyrating round it. The speculative capitalists who had hitherto relied on their power to manipulate one party or another, as the occasion might arise, were thoroughly alarmed. At the previous election, Mr. Blaine had endeavoured to rally the Protectionist interests to the support of the Republicans; but neither party had paid much attention to the subject of tariff. The Democrats claimed to win on the bad character of their opponents rather than upon any definite programme. In 1888 it became necessary to speak out, and the Democratic platform was mainly an echo of the message of 1887. On the other side, the protected manufacturers immediately raised large subscriptions, and sent out agents to organize resistance to this formidable movement. In the declaration adopted at Chicago a few weeks after the nomination of Mr. Cleveland, the Republicans described themselves as "uncompromisingly in favour of the American system of Protection." "We protest against its destruction as proposed by the President and his party: they serve the interests of Europe; we will support the interests of America."

The ill fortune of Mr. Blaine in 1884 made the party unwilling to risk their cause under his leadership a second time, and he went on a visit to Europe, leaving the care of his interests to lieutenants on the spot. The object of the Republican managers was to bring the Western farmers into line with the Protectionists of the Eastern States. The votes of the latter were assured to the party irrespective of the candidate, and it was agreed that a selection should be made from the West. The Convention finally adopted General Benjamin Harrison of Indiana. This gentleman recalled the military glories of the Republicans in the War. After retiring from the army, he attained some distinction at the Bar, and went through a round of political work—serving on Conventions, and for one term as senator for Indiana. His name was of good omen to a party in opposition, for he was the grandson of that General William Harrison whose election to the Presidency in 1840 interrupted, during a few months, the long supremacy of the Democrats.

In the midst of the struggle occurred one of those strange incidents to which all human organization is subject. The English Minister at Washington was addressed by a Mr. Murchison, who, writing from a distant part of the Union, described himself as indifferent to American parties, but with English sympathies. He sought advice how to bestow his vote at the coming election. He professed to be much scandalized at the later declarations of the President in reference to Canada. In a generous moment—a diplomatist ought never to be generous—the Minister replied confidentially, expressing a favourable opinion of the dispositions of the Democratic party towards England, and adding, "allowances must be made for the political situation, as regards the Presidential election."

On the 24th October, just fifteen days before the poll, this correspondence was suddenly published in Republican papers as conclusive evidence that Mr. Cleveland was the creature of the wicked Englishman who is so familiar a figure in American oratory.

The President at once requested Lord Salisbury to recall Sir Sackville West, and as there was no immediate reply to this peremptory demand, "he took a second step which," in the language of Mr. Hensel, "somewhat astonished and baffled Great Britain." *

"On October 30th, six days after the publication of the letter, he notified Minister West that his presence in Washington, as the representative of Great Britain to this country, was no longer agreeable to this Government, and directed that his passports should be delivered to him.

"This decisive action cut the Gordian knot of the difficulty. The British lion now found a tongue, and denounced this action as marked by undue haste and a lack of international courtesy. The President, however, was resolute. . . . . But Great Britain's rulers kept up a show of irritation, and, as punishment to this upstart nation, refused to send a Minister to the United States during the remainder of the Cleveland administration—a deprivation which this country bore with philosophical fortitude and equanimity."

From the point of view of an American public man, it was incumbent on the President, in the unfortunate circumstances, to make some emphatic demonstration. It was, on the other hand, impossible for a foreign Government to treat the exigencies of American electioneering as an excuse for a total disregard of the habits of deliberation essential to international relations.

Mr. Cleveland's position prevented him from taking any direct part in the campaign. General Harrison made 94 speeches in the course of the autumn, and, devoting special attention to his own State, succeeded in securing its 15 votes. This victory in Indiana, coupled with the

* HENSEL'S *Life of Grover Cleveland*, p. 300.

success of the Protectionists in Mr. Cleveland's own State, New York, restored the Republicans to power. The defection of New York from Mr. Cleveland was accounted for in various ways. Some attributed it to the discontent of the Independents at the failure of Mr. Cleveland to carry out their opinions in connection with Civil Service Reform ; others to the hostility of Tammany Hall. That body, it was alleged, had, in the Presidential poll, exchanged the votes of their supporters against Republican votes for certain State offices. The true explanation, however, seems to be that Protectionist combinations showed in defence of their interests unexampled energy and address, and were lavish in their expenditure of money, whilst the Democrats lacked organization.

The growth of Mr. Cleveland in the estimation of the country was illustrated by the fact that, although he lost the Presidency by the votes of the electors chosen by the States, he had a largely increased majority in the vote of the whole country. There is no similar instance of this operation of the mode of election by delegates from States, with the exception of the struggle between Mr. Tilden and Mr. Hayes in 1876, when the Democrats were finally defeated on technical grounds, but had a considerable majority of the vote of the whole nation, reckoned on the plan of a plebiscite.

It was not for personal aims that the President had assailed the huge system of taxation built up in the interest of capitalists ; and in his final message the following month, he returned to the topic discussed in the message of the previous year, and made another vigorous attack upon the tariff. He referred to the approaching centennial anniversary of the Constitution, and contrasted the frugality of the plain people of 1789 with the wealth and luxury of American cities at the present time, whilst "millions are exacted from the citizens to lie unused in the Treasury," and "millions more are added to the cost of living of the people, in order to swell the profits of a small, but powerful, minority." His survey of the state of the Treasury in this his last year of office, is worth recording in view of subsequent events. The total revenue of the year was nearly $8,000,000 larger than in 1887; whilst the expenditure, notwithstanding an increase of $5,000,000 for pensions, was $8,000,000 less. The surplus on the year, apart from the sinking fund, was $119,600,000; and, after payments in purchase of bonds, there remained at the opening of Congress a net surplus of $52,000,000. At the same time, careful management had produced considerable reduction in current expenditure. For instance, the cost of Customs collection was reduced by nearly one per cent.,* whilst many useless offices were abolished.

The most notable measure of this last session was the Direct Tax Refunding Bill. This was another example of the policy of making away with the surplus in the Treasury, in order to escape any demand for reducing the duties. The want of principle, characteristic of Congressional politicians, was shown in the fact that the bill was passed by a House of Representatives in which there was still a majority for the party who had

---

* In 1885 this was 3.77 per cent. It was 2.98 in 1888.

in November been appealing to the country to support them in reducing the tariff.

In August, 1861, when President Lincoln was preparing for war with the Southern States, and the Government was in urgent need of money, Congress had levied a direct tax of $20,000,000 throughout the Union. The loyal States collected and paid their shares, but some four millions of the amount due from the Confederate States had never been paid. An agitation had been on foot for some time to return the amount paid to each of the States, with a view to its distribution among the original taxpayers. It was vain to point out that the tax was a perfectly legitimate one, involving no more oppression or hardship than any other impost of similar amount; and that, as regards the people who had paid, the greater number of them were dead, or not to be found. The bill offered a means of reducing the surplus by so many millions; the donation was welcome to the various State Treasuries; and might give employment to a number of active persons, like the pension agents, whose business Mr. Cleveland had so unkindly interfered with. When the bill was presented for the President's approval, a few days before he retired from office, he declared it to be unconstitutional. Congress could only appropriate money for certain definite purposes set out in the Constitution. There was no "debt due" to the people who had paid the tax; such an appropriation was not for the "public defence," nor could a "sheer bald gratuity, bestowed either upon States or upon individuals," be said to be for "the public welfare." The money which it was proposed to pay away had been contributed by citizens, many of whom were not born when the direct tax was first levied; these people had the first claim upon the existing surplus if it was necessary to get rid of it.

On surrendering office to General Harrison, Mr. Cleveland determined to resume the pursuit of his profession, and took chambers at 816, Madison Avenue, New York. There he entered into partnership, according to the American system, with the firm of Bangs, Stetson, Tracy, and McVeagh. Mr. Hensel tells us he had secured, by his professional savings and judicious investments, a competent fortune; and his practice soon produced a considerable income, which, however, would have been larger, had he not made it a rule to refuse retainers from the great financial and railway corporations.* He found ample employment in the business of arbitrations, whilst he became popular in the artistic and intellectual circles of New York.

It was at this time that his friends induced him to seek opportunities for indulging in his favourite amusement of fishing, at Buzzard's Bay, instead of in the Adirondacks; and he became the occupant of the residence known as "Gray Gables," where he was the neighbour of Mr. Jefferson, the celebrated actor. His visits to this place for fishing and duck shooting secured occasional relaxation from the labours of professional life.

With the purely local politics of the city of New York he scrupulously avoided any connection, but he did not affect unwillingness to take his share in public

* HENSEL's *Cleveland* pp. 319, 320.

life. The fact that he had been President did not, in his view, add to his authority, or discharge him from his public duties. In a speech at Sandwich, Massachusetts, he ridiculed the people who "are greatly disturbed every time an ex-President ventures to express an opinion upon any subject. Not a few appear to think we should simply exist, and be blind, deaf, and dumb the remainder of our days."[*] At a banquet given in his honour by the Democratic Club of New York, he re-affirmed his theory of Democratic policy. "It insists," he tells us, "upon that equality before the law which concedes the care and protection of the Government to simple manhood and citizenship." From this affirmation of Jeffersonian principles, he proceeded to contrast the history of the party with the shiftiness of the Republicans, and concluded an eloquent declaration of faith in the party with the following reference to the recent election:

"We know that we have not deceived the people with false promises or pretences, and we know that we have not corrupted and betrayed the poor with the money of the rich."

At Boston, Philadelphia, and other places, he from time to time delivered important speeches which cheered the spirits of his followers. Of the manifestoes published by him whilst out of office the most celebrated was that of February, 1891, when the advocates for the free coinage of silver were actively pressing their schemes. He was invited to attend a meeting at the Reform Club, New York, and, obliged to send a refusal, on account of

* *Cleveland's Writings and Speeches*, p. 548.

other engagements, he added, "It surely cannot be necessary for me to make a formal expression of my agreement with those who believe that the greatest peril would be invited by the adoption of the scheme embraced in the measure, now pending in Congress, for the unlimited coinage of silver at our mints." He went on to denounce "the dangerous and reckless experiment of free, unlimited, and independent silver coinage." There was nothing in the letter that might not have been expected from him as a matter of course, in view of the language of his speeches and messages on currency, but this declaration was received with wild enthusiasm. So familiar were the public with the trimming of ordinary political leaders, that amidst their dismay at the foolishness of the silver party, they hailed this simple, manly declaration as a promise of safety. "The silver letter" probably did more to ensure his success at the polls in 1892 than anything he had said or done since his retirement from office. The nation rejoiced to have among them a man of great position, who did not spend his time watching which way the winds of popularity were blowing, but, having formed his own opinion, had the courage to avow it.

CHAPTER X.

ELECTION FOR A SECOND TERM.

Questions before the country—Legislation during the Harrison Presidency—The Sherman Act—The McKinley Act—Dependent Pension Act—Great defeat of Republicans at election of Congress in 1890—Disappearance of Surplus—Party platforms—Sudden resignation of Mr. Blaine—Nominations of Harrison and Cleveland—Re-election of Cleveland—Inaugural address—New Cabinet.

WHEN 1892 opened, all the signs of the political sky were in favour of a Democratic triumph. In the fifty-second Congress, which was then in its first session, the Republicans could only claim eighty-eight members out of a total of three hundred and thirty-two, so complete had been the reaction against the Harrison-Blaine administration at the election of 1890.

In order to understand the suddenness of this change after 1888, and the issues which were involved in the next Presidential contest, it will be necessary to glance briefly at the course of events whilst Mr. Cleveland had been devoting himself to his law business in Madison Avenue. General Harrison had been selected for the Presidential office on the ground of his personal popularity in Indiana, and his blameless character: most attractive of all his recommendations was his being a man of whom the professional politicians had no fears. He was not likely to disregard the views of the people who had brought him to Washington. With them would rest the charge of administration. Senator Sherman lost no time in warning him against the evil example of his predecessor. In a letter of congratulation he said :*

"The President should 'touch elbows' with Congress; he should have no policy distinct from that of his party; and this is better represented in Congress than in the Executive. Cleveland made his cardinal mistake in dictating a tariff policy to Congress. Grant also failed to cultivate friendly relations with Congress, and was constantly thwarted by it."

Mr. Blaine, on his return from Europe, became Secretary of State. Thus, in General Harrison's eventful administration, the dominating mind was the orator from Maine, whose struggle with Mr. Cleveland in 1884 has already been narrated. His principal aims in office were to secure appointments for his followers, and acquire popularity by an ambitious foreign policy. In pursuance of the latter object, he wrote, when Secretary to Mr. Garfield, a number of despatches, which asserted for the Union a predominant position in all affairs connected with the American Continent, and the islands in both oceans; although, in relation to the islands, the exact nature of the authority claimed, or the geographical limits of it, had never been defined. In development of this policy came the appointment of Mr. Egan to Valparaiso, and the countenance given to the intervention of that minister in the struggle between the constitutional party in Chili and the dictator Balmaceda. These incidents showed the length to which he was

* SHERMAN, *Recollections*, p. 1032.

prepared to go. The proposed annexation of Hawaii was another example of his schemes of expansion.

As regards home affairs, the Republicans enjoyed, in 1889 and 1890, an advantage which had not fallen to Mr. Cleveland. When the 51st Congress met, in December, 1889, the Protectionist interests, which had excluded Mr. Cleveland from a second term, boasted a majority of seventeen in the House, and of ten in the Senate; and they had the sympathy of the President. The use they made of this opportunity is a remarkable page in American history.

The condition of the currency had become worse since November, and President Harrison, in his message, admitted that "the size of the surplus" demanded the immediate attention of Congress, with a view to reduce the receipts as closely as possible to the needs of the Government. A revision of the tariff was suggested. At the same time, he renewed his profession of faith in Protection, and advised that it should be extended to agricultural industries. The danger from the accumulation of silver dollars was recognized. In the same message, Congress was advised to pass a Dependent Pension Bill, which Mr. Cleveland had vetoed; to remove the excise on tobacco; and to grant subsidies to education. Mr. Reed, of Maine, a man of great determination, was elected Speaker; and it was soon evident that he and his party were resolved to use their majority vigorously, and to guard the tariff system in the future against any arguments founded on the accumulations in the Treasury. The Committee of Ways and Means, to the Chairmanship of which Mr. Reed had appointed Major

McKinley, took up the Senate Bill of the previous Congress. This measure, whilst in name one for the reduction of duties, in reality enacted higher duties on a vast number of articles, for which Protectionists desired to secure an exclusive market.

In order to carry a new tariff, it was necessary to come to some understanding with the champions of silver, who, in this Congress, commanded a substantial majority in the Senate. . That chamber adopted the free coinage of silver, but the bill was defeated in the House of Representatives. Then, after a conference between the two Houses, the silver men were appeased by an act (the Sherman Act, 12th July, 1890), which considerably increased the quantity of silver to be purchased each month by the Treasury.* The purpose of this measure was to secure the passage of the larger scheme, then slowly proceeding through Congress, the famous McKinley Act.

These two measures were the reply of the Protectionists to the tariff message in the previous Congress. The exertions of Mr. Cleveland had induced the House of Representatives, in 1888, to adopt a scheme for the reduction of the tariff, the Mills Tariff Bill. In 1890 the Republicans raised the duties on a vast number of articles, amongst others on wool, clothing, and steel rails, The capitalist, who had a bounty out of the taxes on his fellow citizens, felt the necessity of adding buttresses to his structure, and proceeded to give a symmetrical aspect to the tariff system established during the War. Had it not been for the message of 1887, Protectionists

* See upon this Act chapter xi. p. 161.

would probably have left things as they were; but, alarmed by Mr. Cleveland, they pressed on, both to raise the more important duties and impose new ones, in order to win support from other classes. In many cases duties were increased so as not only to limit but practically to exclude importations. The tariff policy was no longer a defensive one, as Mr. Blaine had presented it in 1884. It was not enough to protect existing manufactures against foreign competition. Taxes were to be levied for the purpose of creating new branches of business. Senator Sherman declared in the Senate, "Whenever a new industry can be started in our country with a successful hope of living . . . we ought to establish it." *

Of the new policy, the duty on tinplates is a familiar illustration. This was not an article manufactured in the States. In 1883 a duty of 30 per cent. had been levied on importations, but such a rate was not sufficient to stimulate the production of tinplates at home. The McKinley Act raised the duty to 70 per cent., adding a provision that it should be abolished altogether in 1896, unless, in the meantime, the home product of tinplates rose to one-third of the importations.

The tax on raw sugar was abolished, for it was a revenue tax, only about one-tenth of the sugar consumed being of home manufacture. This provision served the double purpose of reducing the surplus by some $50,000,000 a year, and of winning popularity for the Administration in those parts of the country not con-

* SHERMAN, *Recollections,* p. 1086.

cerned with manufacturing industry. By way of helping agriculture, as President Harrison had suggested, duties were imposed, or those already existing were raised, on wheat, Indian corn, barley, flax, potatoes, eggs, and wool; but as there was hardly any importation of these articles, with the exception of barley, the alteration, as regards agricultural products, had no effect either upon trade or revenue. They were merely an effort to persuade the farmer that Congress was ready to help him out of the taxes as well as the manufacturer.

A popular part of the Act was the reciprocity scheme, which enabled the President, by proclamation, to impose duties on sugar and other commodities (nearly all the produce of South American countries) if he found that any countries exporting these commodities to the States levied unreasonable duties on American produce.

Mr. Windom, the Secretary of the Treasury, described this measure from the Republican point of view.

"The area of population, the accumulated wealth and characteristic resources of the United States, render it certain that, for many years to come, the home market will be a better one for our own products than all others combined. This very superiority of the United States as a market, is an inducement to foreign producers everywhere to seek access to and control of it. To permit our own producers to be driven out by foreign competition, would be to expel them from their best and most natural market, and compel them to seek inferior competitive markets elsewhere. Free trade can never be successfully established, or perpetuated, in any country whose home market for its own products exceeds its aggregate markets abroad." *

* *House Exec. Docs.* 51st Cong. vol. xix. p. 33.

Mr. Windom's theory of including the States within
a sort of ring fence, was defended on the ground that
home competition would prevent the local producer from
having any unfair advantage over the consumer. Whilst
the act was under discussion, associations of manufacturers were formed throughout the country, with
the view of crushing competition; and these Trusts, or
Companies, excited the apprehension of the whole
community.

In the same session Congress passed the Dependent
Pension Bill, under the provisions of which, $30,000,000
additional expenditure was incurred. Liberal appropriations, too, were made for public works. By these devices
the Republicans secured one object: the country would
no more be troubled with the argument against high
tariff founded on recurring surpluses.

The McKinley Act came into operation on October
1st, 1890, and the immediate result was a general rise in
price at the retail stores throughout the country. For
every article of consumption the dealer asked more
money. At the same time importers waited to see the
result. Many branches of the import trade were stopped
altogether. Speculative enterprise was directed rather to
secure high profits to existing business concerns than to
start new industries.

The election of Congress, which occurred the next
month, supplied an extraordinary example of the in-
stability of popular majorities. The Republicans had
worked very hard for their victory in 1888. They had
given many reckless pledges, but with the help of Mr.
Reed they had fully carried them out. The specu-

lative capitalist had attained his ends. He had exacted payment for his subscriptions and his vote in the shape of the McKinley Act. The rise in prices was general, whilst there was no improvement in wages or salaries. The elector began to think seriously what he was about. General Harrison and Major McKinley had told him in 1888 that cheapness was English and mean, and he voted for a spirited American policy; but when dearness came, he failed to recognize it as a national blessing. It was believed that the rise in prices was only beginning. In many branches of manufacture production ceased, owing to the increased cost of materials, and capitalists hesitated to avail themselves of the opportunity for starting new industries. The change had been so sweeping that they wished to see how it would work before investing their money. When the polling day came the Democrats won all along the line. In New England and the Middle States the Democratic vote was not high, but the Republican vote was reduced by nearly a third; whilst in the West, crowds, who had voted for Harrison in 1888, returned to the Democrats in 1890. Major McKinley himself lost his seat in Ohio, and the Republican party returned to Washington mustering eighty-five less than in the previous Congress. Sanguine people declared that the process of education which Mr. Cleveland had begun by his message of 1887 had at last succeeded.

Towards the close of President Harrison's term, the financial outlook became still more gloomy. Silver continued to fall in price, and whilst the issue of the new currency, the silver certificates, went on each month, the public refused to keep either these or the Bland silver dollars. They were all sent to the Treasury to be exchanged for gold, or greenbacks payable in gold, and the export to Europe of that metal steadily increased. The abundant crops of 1890, and the high price of produce in Europe, had, for a time, caused an influx of gold; but in 1892 there was a sudden advance in gold exports, and much anxiety as to the future prevailed in all financial centres.

It was in these circumstances that the Conventions of the two parties met in June. That of the Republicans on the 7th, at Minneapolis, was preceded by an incident characteristic of their ambitious leader. It had been announced for some time past that the Secretary of State no longer desired the Presidency, and that President Harrison would seek nomination for a second term. Suddenly, three days before the meeting of the Convention, Mr. Blaine resigned office as head of General Harrison's Cabinet, and appeared as a candidate.

The Republican platform was much less aggressive on the subject of tariff than in former years. The claim for high duties did not extend to all goods consumed in America, but to imports coming into competition with the products of American labour. As regards silver, bimetallism was applauded, and the proposal for an international conference advocated; but nothing was said about free coinage, or the claims of American mine-owners on the sympathy of their countrymen. The party affirmed the Monroe doctrine, and their belief in "the achievement of the manifest destiny of the Republic in its broadest sense." Notwithstanding the suddenness of Mr. Blaine's swoop upon the Convention, the supporters of General Harrison held their ground, and, after two days spent in balloting, secured his nomination.

The Democrats were more outspoken: they denounced the McKinley Act as "the culminating atrocity of class legislation," the tariff system as "a robbery of the great majority of the people for the benefit of the few," and pledged themselves to its repeal. The Sherman Act was described as fraught with possibilities of danger in the future, which should make all anxious to see it abolished. As to foreign affairs, they repudiated "a policy of irritation and bluster, which is liable at any time to confront us with the alternatives of humiliation or war."

The popularity of the Democrats, it was universally admitted, was not due so much to anything that the party had done in opposition, as to the contrast between General Harrison and Mr. Cleveland. The silver and tariff interests had run away with the Republican majorities in the previous Congress, and the President had made no attempt to check their wild career. The country thought, with pride, of the different attitude President Cleveland had adopted during his tenure of office—how resolutely he had maintained his own line of policy, in spite of mutiny within his party, and the unscrupulous opposition of the Republicans. Public opinion designated him as the candidate for 1892, even before the preparations for the National Convention were begun. The wire-pullers, however, were much more active than in 1888. Besides their personal dislike of a leader who had not graduated in their political school, tradition discouraged the giving the nomination to a man who had once been defeated. Tactical considerations, however, had no weight with the mass of the delegates. , Their own observation showed them the general current of national sentiment, and the first ballot gave him an overwhelming majority, in spite of the exertions of old political hands. He was the candidate not so much of the party as of the nation.

The most amusing characteristic of this contest was the continual appeal of the Republicans to the wealth of the country. When they were unable to get over the evidence that Protection, on the scale of the act of 1890, was very costly, their reply was, "Cannot we afford it?" "Are not we the richest nation in the world?" and if they were reminded that gold was flowing away to the old countries that loved cheapness, they told the voter that this was only the craft of the gold standard people. These conspirators withdrew gold in order to deter Americans from relying on the illimitable source of wealth which the silver mines supplied.

The inaugural ceremony on the following fourth of March had not that special significance which attended the installation of a Democratic President in 1884, but it was much more of a personal triumph for Mr. Cleveland. In the recent election he was pre-eminently representative of the one-man power, as cherished by Democrats. He had been called back to office because the nation believed in his courage and honesty; although, according to all the notions of professional politicians, a President who had failed to obtain a second term was no longer in public life.

His address at the Capitol was a business-like message

to Congress, rather than the usual array of personal reflections. He began by reminding his audience of the duties which the late election had imposed upon the Legislature. The struggle had not been between one leader and another, or even between the two parties. The country had asked to be delivered from the politicians who had worked the legislative machinery in the interest of the speculative owner of capital.

"The verdict of our voters which condemned the injustice of maintaining Protection for Protection's sake, enjoins upon the people's servants the duty of exposing and destroying the brood of kindred evils which are the unwholesome progeny of paternalism."*

He proceeded to impress upon his followers the obligations which had been imposed upon them by their success.

"The people of the United States have decreed that on this day the control of their government in its legislative and executive branches, shall be given to a political party pledged in the most positive terms to the accomplishment of tariff reform. They have thus determined in favour of a more just and equitable system of Federal taxation. The agents they have chosen to carry out their purposes are bound by their promises, not less than by the command of their masters, to devote themselves unremittingly to this service."

This appeal to the party to apply themselves to the work before them had a special significance, and recalled the history of the contest in November. Congress had been elected to carry out the policy of which Mr. Cleveland traced the lines four years before. Those principles were affirmed by the nation in 1890, but to the Congress then

* *Congressional Record*, 1093, vol. 25, p. 3.

L

chosen the Executive was adverse. Now the nation had recalled Cleveland to office and sent him a Congress pledged to his policy. The Democratic majority was not so numerous as in 1890, but it was large, and principally made up of men who in the fifty-second Congress had declared for reduction of tariff.

The inauguration being over, the next business was the choice of a Cabinet. On this occasion Mr. Cleveland departed from the plan he had adopted in his first term. Then it was his object to show that a satisfactory Administration could be formed out of the Democratic party. This time he turned to Mr. Gresham, of Illinois, who had been long regarded as the representative of Independent opinion among the Republicans. He was proposed as the candidate of the party in the election of 1888, but received no support from the political managers. He became Secretary of State, whilst Mr. Carlisle, of Kentucky, who had done distinguished service as Speaker in the previous Congress, went to the Treasury. Mr. Carlisle, in the early part of his career, was not quite free from the inflationist heresies which exercise so great an attraction upon many Democrats; but the arguments of Mr. Cleveland had gradually convinced him of the danger arising from concessions to the silver interest, and all through the second Cleveland Presidency he has contended against that movement with vigour and ability. Mr. Hoke Smith, of Georgia, as Secretary of the Interior, and Mr. H. A. Herbert, of Alabama, as Secretary of the Navy, represented the South. From New York came Mr. Lamont, as Secretary of War, and Mr. W. S. Bissel, as Postmaster - General;

whilst from the New England Democrats, Mr. Olney was selected for the office of Attorney General. Mr. J. Stirling Morton, of Nebraska, was appointed to the Commissionership of Agriculture, a department to which Mr. Cleveland had, in his first Administration, given Cabinet rank.

Of Mr. Cleveland's former ministers, Mr. Manning was dead, Mr. Lamar had accepted a seat in the Supreme Court, Mr. Bayard proceeded as Ambassador to St. James'. The new Administration did not include a single member of the old Cabinet.

The drain of gold which had excited alarm in the previous year continued all through the spring, and it was reported that the President would exercise the power which the Constitution gave him of calling Congress together for the despatch of business, immediately after his installation. It has been said since that, had he taken this course in March, he might have been able to shape the new Congress to his policy, and would have had a much better account to render of Democratic administration. By postponing the meeting of Congress, he gave time for the intrigues of various self-seeking politicians, who might have been cowed if called on to fulfil their pledges whilst the President's laurels were still fresh from the triumph of popular vote. These critics, however, overlook the fact that an interval of four months between the election and opening of Congress was inevitable; and this was undoubtedly used in arranging various combinations in the Senate to thwart the cause of the new Administration. In considering such speculations we must keep in mind that the difficulties he encountered were not in the House of Representatives, which, on the whole, acted with public spirit and loyalty towards him, but in the Senate ; and it seems doubtful whether any degree of promptitude would have disarmed the antagonism of the Gormans and the Brices. The President perhaps saw that, with obstacles of this kind before him, it was impossible for a new Cabinet, whose members had not yet made themselves acquainted with the records of their respective departments, to enter immediately upon a course of drastic legislation. The formal session of the Senate for the sanction of the new appointments concluded without any announcement as to the date of meeting for general business, and the power to call Congress together in extra session was not exercised until August.

CHAPTER XI.

CURRENCY LEGISLATION.

Extra session of Congress—Review of the Silver movement—
Republican finance during the War—Popularity of greenbacks—
Desire for abundant currency—Resumption Act, 1875—Rise of
the Silver interest—The Bland Act—Cleveland proposes its repeal,
1885 — The Sherman Act, 1890 — Monetary Crisis of 1893 —
Cleveland proposes repeal of the Sherman Act—Obstruction in
the Senate—Repeal carried.

THE events of the next few months made it clear
that the aid of legislation was urgently needed,
and an extraordinary session was summoned for the
7th August. Before detailing the proposals which the
President laid before Congress, it will be necessary
to glance at the history of American currency. The
career of the silver interest brings out very vividly
the susceptibility of American politics to speculative
impulses, and the struggle of Cleveland against the
aggressions of the mine-owners will stand out as one
of the most memorable incidents in his career.

A very dramatic chapter in the annals of the Republic
is the destruction of the Bank of the United States by
President Jackson. However deficient that statesman
may have been in economic knowledge, he gave practical
effect to an idea popular with the Democratic party.

149

The control of the currency by any single corporation they regarded as dangerous to the principle of equality, and tending to the establishment of a centralized system of government. It is not necessary here to go into that story, or the subsequent experiments with State Banks, and the disasters which ensued. The ultimate result of Jackson's policy was that the United States Treasury combined with its ordinary functions of collecting and expending the national revenue, the further duties of banker to the nation. When the Civil War obliged the Government to make large issues of paper money, this banking business assumed vast proportions, the issue of paper currency being under the control of the Treasury. When peace came, the great object of financiers was to get rid of the depreciated paper, and gradually bring the country back to the use of gold. The Resumption Act, passed in 1875, prescribed that the Government should be ready to pay all the notes of the United States in coin, on or at any time after January 1st, 1879. For this purpose the Treasury was authorized to accumulate coin over and above what was required to meet the national expenses, and this hoard was to remain as a store, out of which the public might be supplied in exchange for notes. At this time there was no silver in circulation, whilst the coin required for settlement of foreign accounts was gold. The Treasury came to the conclusion that coin meant gold coin, and that the accumulation prescribed ought never to be less than $100,000,000. From the rule of practice thus introduced, has grown up the theory that there must always be in the custody of the Department the amount of $100,000,000 in gold over and above current liabilities. The rule as to the particular sum, although nowhere directly enjoined by act of Congress, was subsequently recognized in legislation, and is now an essential part of the Treasury system. It will be seen later on that the business of keeping up the gold reserve amidst the disorders produced by the believers in an abundant currency, and the champions of silver, has been the most onerous task imposed upon Mr. Cleveland during his second term.

One effect of the lavish issues of paper during the Civil War, was to drive coin of all descriptions out of the country. Even before the War, gold being more abundant than silver in consequence of the discoveries in California, silver had disappeared, and the unit for the settlement of all accounts was the gold dollar. With the altered condition of public affairs in 1862, a new financial policy was introduced. The Government had to provide for an enormous increase of expenditure, and they adopted four different expedients. They established a system of internal taxation, applicable to incomes and to everything used by the public; they laid heavy duties on all imports; they adopted a paper currency of two kinds; and they raised loans at various rates of interest.

It is the measures coming under these two latter heads that demand our attention here. Many millions of notes, commonly called greenbacks, were issued in the name of the United States. These notes were of different denominations—from one dollar upwards—and were made available for all public and private payments, except import duties and interest on the National Debt. The import duties were to be paid in gold, and the revenue derived from them was pledged for payment of interest on the new loans, and a contribution of one per cent. for a sinking fund. Thus a basis of gold was secured, in order to attract loans from foreign countries; whilst all home transactions were being conducted in paper. In addition to the United States notes, or greenbacks, there were other notes issued to the public, by a new organization of local banks called National Banks. These institutions were authorized by the Treasury to circulate bank-notes to the amount of ninety per cent. of such Government bonds as the banks chose to deposit with the Treasury. By this expedient a market was at once created for the bonds in different parts of the country, and the populations of distant localities acquired a direct personal concern in the outcome of the struggle. These notes might be paid to the Government, or to other banks, and every bank was bound to change them for greenbacks, but they were not a forced currency available for payment of debts between individuals. When the War came to an end, there was outstanding a sum of $454,218,000 in United States notes, besides over $350,000,000 of National Bank notes; and the gold required for purposes of foreign trade was at a high premium.

In order to get rid of this premium, the Resumption Act of 1875 enjoined that the Secretary of the Treasury should gradually reduce the amount of greenbacks in circulation to $300,000,000, and this process was commenced. Then, owing to the vicissitudes of business after the War, the theory sprang up that an inflated currency was in itself a good thing. The greenback currency was associated, in the minds of the people, with high wages and brisk business, and was supposed to be a means of enlarging and adding to the material prosperity of the people throughout the country. This opinion became so general, that a distinct party organization was started; and the attempt was made, in 1880 and in 1884, to elect a President and Congress pledged to maintain the greenback issue, and make these notes legal tender in all cases. "We want," said the Greenback Convention of 1884, "that money which saved our country in time of war, and which has given it prosperity and happiness in peace."

In May, 1878, an act was passed to prevent the further cancellation of these notes. The provision made in 1875 for paying gold to all who demanded it was not interfered with; but the Secretary of the Treasury was directed to go on issuing greenbacks as fast as they came in, and under this enactment there are now $346,000,000 of these notes still in circulation.

Before the date for resuming payment in coin came round, a new force had come into play, in comparison with which the crotchets of the greenback party were insignificant. Vast deposits of silver had been discovered in the Far West, and the increased output of that metal attracted attention all over the world. The prejudice in favour of plentiful currency, and apprehension as to the effect of the resumption of payment in specie on remote localities, where the system of credit was not fully organized—these notions afforded the shareholders in the

Comstock and Virginia mines, and similar stores, a favourable opportunity.

A great silver-mining trade had been growing in all the States along the Rocky Mountains. The annual product of this metal within the Union at the commencement of the Civil War was $2,000,000. In 1873 it had risen to $36,500,000. Here, when people were beginning to talk of the want of more currency, was disclosed a magnificent —almost illimitable—supply of that metal, which had served as the material of monetary exchange in every part of the world for thousands of years. If manufacturing industries were to be encouraged by legislation, why should not extractive industries also have their turn? The people would have an abundance of what was supposed to be a guarantee of wealth, and American owners would get the benefit of the demand.

Accordingly, an outcry for the use of silver arose in many directions. To encourage this new industry was the natural disposition of the American people; and this tendency was stimulated when the public were reminded that the silver dollar had been, in former years, the standard of value. It was only by the Mint Act of 1873, at a time when there was no metallic currency in the country, when, as Senator Sherman tells us, the silver dollar was "not a known coin," that Congress, in preparing for the scheme of resuming coin payments, abolished the free coinage of silver, practically substituting a gold standard for the old silver standard.

An additional incitement to making the best of the opportunity which the state of American opinion presented, was the condition of the silver market in Europe.

Germany had, soon after the French War, reduced silver to the same subsidiary position which it occupied in England. In a few years the Latin Union ceased to coin this metal for the unlimited payment of debts.

Whilst the output of silver was continually increasing, and the supply " in sight " exceeded all calculations, European countries were showing a strange indifference to these blessings. An appeal to American patriotism might, it was hoped, do something to redress this neglect, and the theories of the inflationist party supplied a favourable soil for the proposal to create a national currency from bullion obtained at home.

The Democratic party had many connections with the new States of the Rocky Mountains, and, being in opposition, had some temptations to welcome the new movement. It has been mainly the personal influence of Mr. Cleveland that for so long a time has prevented the silver owners from getting possession of the machinery of the party. *

It is not necessary here to examine the controversy between Bi-metallism and Mono-metallism. President Cleveland's struggle has been with the owners of silver, who, having acquired great sources of wealth in Nevada and other Western States, immediately demanded that their political representatives should give an artificial value to their commodity. In so doing, the miners of the Rocky Mountains have only followed that prevailing habit, which can be traced all through American history. It was what the owners of black labour did in the first part of the century; what the manufacturing interests which sprang

* See p. 238 as to Chicago Convention of July, 1896.

up during the war of 1814 have persistently attempted, and what they secured on the outbreak of the Civil War.

In November, 1887, when the price of silver had fallen ten per cent., Mr. Bland, Democrat, of Missouri, in a Democratic House of Representatives, suddenly carried through the preliminary stages a bill to restore the free coinage of the old silver dollar, and make it unlimited legal tender.

The result of Mr. Bland's exertions was a bill which did not, as originally proposed, establish free coinage, but which directed the Treasury to purchase not less than $2,000,000 of silver per month, nor more than $4,000,000, and have it coined monthly—"as fast as so purchased"—into dollars. These dollars were to be legal tender "for all debts and dues, public and private, except where otherwise expressly stipulated in the contract." In order to get over the difficulty arising from the bulkiness of this metal, any holders of dollars might deposit them at the Treasury, and obtain in exchange certificates which were receivable for Customs, taxes, and all public dues, but were not unlimited legal tender for private debts.

President Hayes interposed his veto, but the bill was carried by the requisite two-thirds majority, 28th February, 1878.*

---

* Mr. Sherman's account of his own attitude at this time is characteristic of Congressional politics. As Secretary to the Treasury, he was the most responsible adviser of the President and the nation; but he tells us, "In view of the strong public sentiment in favour of the free coinage of the silver dollar, I thought it better to make no objections to the passage of the bill, but I did not care to antagonize the wishes of the President."—*Recollections*, p. 623.

Thus some ten months before the long-desired event, the resumption of specie payments, the conditions under which these payments were to be made were completely altered. In the first place, the great forced loan represented by greenbacks was not to be got rid of, but was to remain outstanding; secondly, the contrivance for securing gold through the Customs House was abandoned; thirdly, Congress made a partial surrender to the great mercantile interest in silver, guaranteeing these people a market for their goods to the extent of at least $24,000,000 a year. The loans of the United States were payable in coin; and a new kind of coin was now created, which many powerful politicians desired, as everyone knew, to substitute for gold. It was a coin of which the bullion value was declining day by day, and it was impossible to say to what uses it might be put by the new leaders of Congress. The immediate result was a severe shock to the credit of the Union, just at the time when it ought to have stood highest. The currency legislation after 1875 produced apprehensions which are gradually undoing that work of redemption of debt carried on with such brilliant success in the years that followed the close of the War.

When Mr. Cleveland assumed office in 1885, the Bland Act had been in operation for over seven years. The Secretary of the Treasury attempted to avail himself of the provisions of the law making the Bland dollars legal tender. He used them in payment of salaries and other Government obligations, but they were immediately brought back to the sub-Treasuries of the Government to be exchanged for gold. These requests the Government did not dare refuse, for fear that the public would become alarmed, and begin to hoard gold as a provision against future difficulties. In November, 1885, $215,759,431 had been coined, and only about a quarter of this amount had got into circulation. Mr. Manning said, "The Mints are full of unissued silver dollars, and the sub-Treasuries of returned silver dollars." * The owners of silver took care to get gold for the bullion which the Treasury was bound to purchase. Thus every month two millions of gold in the public Treasury was paid out. The use of silver in payment of taxes had increased from twenty per cent. to fifty-eight per cent. "If continued long enough," said Mr. Cleveland, "this operation will result in the substitution of silver for all the gold the Government owns applicable to its general purposes. It will not do to rely upon the Customs receipts of the Government to make good this drain of gold. . . . The proportion of silver and its certificates received by the Government will probably increase as time goes on, for the reason that the nearer the period approaches when it will be obliged to offer silver in payment of its obligations, the greater inducement there will be to hoard gold against depreciation in the value of silver, or for the purpose of speculating. . . . It is the ceaseless stream which threatens to overflow the land that causes fear and uncertainty." † As a remedy he suggested the suspension of the compulsory coining of silver.

In a vigorous report for 1884, Mr. Manning reviewed the fiscal history of the country since the close of

* *Treasury Report*, *H. Ex. Docs.* 1884-85.
† *Annual Message*, December, 1885, p. 22.

the War, and in support of the President's demand for relief from the evils produced by "the mixture of private jobs and past public needs," advocated the repeal of the Bland Act, and a reduction of tariff. Whilst other nations were restricting or renouncing the use of silver, the Union had bound itself to take off the market half the produce of its own mines, the theory being that this course might keep up the prices of commodities; but "prices in the United States," said Mr. Manning, "are the record of the fluctuations of commodities and currencies in the market of the world. They are not merely domestic fluctuations. Odessa and India appear in the price of wheat at Chicago. Our legislation chiefly concerns fifty-five millions of people; but prices are the outcome of twelve to fifteen hundred million people's affairs." *

The remedy for declining prices adopted by Congress was to use a currency of which only $8,000,000 had been found necessary during the eighty years that the United States possessed a silver standard. In the eight years which had elapsed since the Bland Act, $215,000,000 had been coined. At the same time, the production of silver in American mines, which in 1881 amounted to 50 per cent. of the world's production, rose in three years to 61 per cent. In such circumstances, the attempt to make the full silver dollar an equivalent in value to the gold dollar was "a highly profitable transaction for the 100,000 silver miners of the United States, but not for the people of more than fifty millions."†

---

* *Treasury Report, H. Ex. Docs.* 1884-85.
† *Treasury Report,* p. 27. 1884-85.

Mr. Fairchild, who succeeded Mr. Manning in 1887, remarked that "large classes of our business men have come to depend for success upon their skill in manipulating Governmental agencies rather than upon industry, intelligence, and honourable competition"; and he closed an admirable review of the situation in 1888 by the following queries, which have a quaint flavour of Bishop Berkeley:

"Can a Government be kept pure and free, which, through the agency of its laws, offers vast pecuniary temptations to some kinds of business?

"Is it not possible that eagerness for the money which men assume comes to them only through Government, may lead them to use an ever-growing portion of their gains to possess and influence the supposed source of their wealth? . . .

"Will not the endeavour to make men rich soon become the chief function of our Government?"*

These entreaties of the President and his Cabinet for a repeal of the Bland Act and a reduction of tariff were renewed again and again, but without success, during the whole four years from 1885–1888. It was not until the exploits of the Harrison-Blaine Administration had thoroughly alarmed the country that the exhortations of Mr. Cleveland prevailed over the speculative interests which had become all powerful in Congress.

Such was the condition of affairs when Mr. Cleveland made way for General Harrison in 1889. The silver owners then renewed their efforts to check the fall in the price of their commodity, and again proposed the free coinage of silver at the old ratio of 16 to 1. As their

* *Treasury Report*, 1887-88. *H. Ex. Docs.* p. 27.

support was needed for the passage of the tariff scheme on which the Republicans had staked their fortunes, it was impossible to refuse them some concessions. For the Bland Act of 1878 was substituted a direction to the Secretary to the Treasury (the Sherman Act, July 12th, 1890) to purchase every month 4,500,000 ounces of silver, and pay for it at the market price of the metal, not in gold, but in Treasury notes of various denominations, from $1 to $1000. These notes, known as "Treasury coin notes," were redeemable on demand in gold or silver coin at the discretion of the Treasury. In committee, the following words were added to the description of them: "It being the established policy of the United States to maintain the two metals on a parity with each other upon the present legal ratio, or such ratio as may be provided by law." In many respects this bill was a boon to the shareholders in silver mines. The principle of compelling Government to keep a market for their metal was again affirmed, and the quantity to be purchased considerably increased, as the Government had never under the Bland Act purchased more than the minimum of $2,000,000 a month.

The Treasury no longer converted the bullion purchased into dollars, but was obliged to accumulate a commodity which was steadily falling in price. The declaration as to the policy of the United States was, however, a formal affirmation of the practice hitherto pursued; and this reflection mitigated the anxiety of the public at the renewed evidence which the Act supplied, of the control of the silver interest over Congress. The Sherman Act did not materially alter the situation, as

M

described by Mr. Manning and Mr. Fairchild, except
that there was added another form of paper currency
which was made legal tender for all purposes. The silver
certificates, under the Bland Bill, were legal tender to
the Government, but not to private creditors. These
"Treasury coin notes" were made available for the
payment of private debts as well as taxes,* and being
redeemable by the Treasury in silver or gold, they, like
greenbacks, have been always, as a matter of course,
paid in gold when the public so required.

Soon after his inauguration, it was Mr. Cleveland's
privilege to preside over the opening of the Columbian
Centenary Exposition. This celebration of five centuries
of achievement, and of one century of national existence,
had been in preparation for some years, and on the first
of May, 1893, East and West, North and South, assembled
at Chicago to pass in proud review the magnificent results
of industry, organization, and invention. The natural
pride of the people at the splendour of the scene had
hardly found expression, before terrible events came to
remind them that neither the vast material resources
of the country, nor the high spirit of the nation, had
brought wisdom or permanent prosperity.

The bullion value of the silver dollar, which had fallen
to 88 cents in July, 1892, continued to decline, and at
the same time the export of gold increased. The
Treasury reserve of $100,000,000, which was formerly
considered only enough to secure the national liability
for some $350,000,000 of greenbacks, had now to sustain
$480,000,000 more of new currency in Treasury notes

---

* Except in cases of express contracts for payment in gold.

and silver certificates. In April there were already signs of the hoarding of gold. There were runs upon many of the country banks, and numerous failures through May and June. Then at the end of the latter month came the closing of the mints of India to the free coinage of silver, and the price of that metal fell to 67. Many mines were closed in Utah and the other silver States. A panic swept over the country: three hundred and one banks suspended payment, and business of every kind was paralyzed. The deposits and other resources of the surviving banks showed a diminution of over four hundred million dollars, and the crisis left effects from which the Union has suffered ever since.

It was in this condition of affairs that, on the 8th August, the President applied to Congress for that relief which he had demanded in vain during his first term of office. The message reviewed the results of the Sherman Act, which he described as a truce between the advocates of free silver coinage, and those who wished for a more conservative policy. He referred to the distrust that prevailed not only in the Union, but among foreign holders of American securities.

" It does not meet the situation to say that apprehension in regard to the future of our finances is groundless, and that there is no reason for lack of confidence in the purposes or power of the Government. The very existence of this apprehension and lack of confidence, however caused, is a menace which ought not for a moment to be disregarded."

He asked for an immediate repeal of the clauses of the Sherman Act authorizing the purchase of silver bullion. A Repeal Bill was promptly introduced in the House of Representatives, carried by a majority of 131, and sent to the Senate before the end of August. In the latter Chamber, however, it remained for two months. There was a majority of about eleven for the bill, but the larger part of its supporters were Republicans, not Democrats; whilst the minority entered upon a course of obstruction for which the previous history of the Senate afforded no parallel. Towards the end of October, 1893, one sitting was continued for fourteen days without interruption. At length this opposition was overcome, and the bill was returned to the House, where Mr. Reed supported it, and it became law on the 1st November. The unscrupulousness of the minority in the Senate showed the extent of the danger to which the country was exposed, for they consisted of professed adherents of the Government. If Mr. Cleveland had achieved nothing else, the resolution with which, on this occasion, he kept his party together in the House against the veterans of the Upper Chamber, would alone secure him the grateful recollection of his countrymen. Several Republicans in the Senate acted with commendable public spirit, but they would have had no inducement to take this course had it not been for the influence which Mr. Cleveland exerted over the Democratic majority in the other Chamber.

CHAPTER XII.

OBSTRUCTION IN THE SENATE.

Second session of the Cleveland Congress—The President's summons to action—Mr. Carlisle on Reduction of Duties—The Wilson Bill —Success in the House—Opposition in the Senate—Letter to Mr. Wilson—Wool duty abolished—The railway strike—Troops of the United States to Chicago—Governor Altgeld—Treasury obliged to purchase gold—Democrats defeated at elections of 1894—Income tax annulled by Supreme Court—President urges the withdrawal of greenbacks, and reform of the bank laws.

THE second part of the policy which the Democratic successes of 1892 had affirmed was reduction of tariff, and this involved a still more protracted contest than that over the Sherman Act, whilst the results were much less definite. After a short recess, the second session of the Cleveland Congress was opened, but the country had to wait nine months before the new Tariff Act was passed, and then it was found not to be a fulfilment of Democratic promises. The session began, however, with the hope of better work. Mr. Cleveland concluded the annual review of foreign affairs and the work of public departments by a spirited appeal to Congress to carry out the pledges of the election.

"After a hard struggle, tariff reform is directly before us. Nothing so important claims our attention, and nothing so clearly presents itself as both an opportunity and a duty—an opportunity to deserve the gratitude of our fellow citizens, and a duty imposed upon us by our oft-repeated professions, and by the emphatic mandate of the people. After full discussion, our countrymen have spoken in favour of this reform, and they have confided the work of its accomplishment to the hands of those who are solemnly pledged to it.

"If there is anything in the theory of a representation in public places of the people and their desires, if public officers are really the servants of the people, and if political promises and professions have any binding force, our failure to give the relief so long awaited will be sheer recreancy." *

Whilst he insisted on the proposition that duties ought not to be levied unless the Government required the money, he added that the state of affairs which previous legislation had brought about called for careful discrimination in the selection of the duties which were retained. Consideration was due to the people who had invested their money in reliance on the policy of Congress. He declared his fiscal policy to be, in the first place, the abolition of duties upon necessaries of life. The change would thus be made perceptible to thousands who would be better fed, better clothed, and better sheltered. His second object was the repeal of all duties on raw materials, and he announced that a bill on these lines had been prepared by the Committee of Ways and Means.

The Treasury Report showed that, so effectually had the surplus of former years been reduced by the Harrison legislation, there was only a balance over of some two million dollars in June. This condition of the finances

* *President's Message,* December, 1893, p. 29.

was one consequence of the McKinley experiment. That wild attempt to change the whole course of trade, and substitute a protected home market for all foreign commerce, had been condemned by acclamation within two months of the passing of the act; but the country was compelled to wait nearly three years before the legislative machinery could be got into working order to apply a remedy. Meanwhile, every kind of business suffered from uncertainty, and the scare about silver added to the depression. Mr. Sherman tells us that it was the election of Mr. Cleveland which did the mischief,* but the trouble had begun before the end of 1890. It was clear, after the election of Congress that year, that the policy of Mr. McKinley was condemned by the country. The only question was how soon the counter system could be introduced. Until March, 1893, Mr. Cleveland and the tariff reformers had had no chance of giving effect to their policy, and the succeeding months had been given up to currency. Mr. Carlisle, on behalf of the Treasury, admitted that the Government needed additional funds to meet public expenditure, and would probably require still more to keep up the gold reserve; but he urged that a wise reduction of the tariff would set the mind of the business world at ease, and give commerce a new start.

The bill referred to by the President was introduced by Mr. Wilson, the Chairman of the Committee of Ways and Means, and was favourably received by the House, which passed it through on the 1st February, 1894. It did not involve any very striking changes,

* SHERMAN, *Recollections*, p. 1203.

except in regard to raw materials.   Wool, coal, and iron were to be admitted free of duty; but duties which were practically prohibitive were retained on partly manufactured goods, such as pig iron and steel billets, whilst the reductions on finished articles were inconsiderable.   It corresponded, in fact, with the pledges which Mr. Cleveland and his supporters had frequently given, that account should be taken of the enterprises which previous legislation had encouraged.   It was not a Free Trade Bill, in the English sense of the term, but it differed altogether from the principles propounded by the McKinleyite following.   It recognized import trade as a source of revenue, instead of seeking to shut out all foreigners from the American market.   The Republicans had succeeded in passing thirty-two Tariff Acts, to aid one calling or another, since their acquisition of power in 1860; and the Wilson Bill was a declaration that the patience of the taxpayer was exhausted.

The proposal of Mr. Carlisle to provide against a deficit, by a tax on the profits of public companies, was converted into a general income tax of two per cent. This change, although apparently made with a view of helping the Treasury, augured ill for the future progress of the measure; but the abolition of duties on raw materials was heartily approved; and the ovation given to Mr. Wilson, on the passage of the bill through the House, was regarded as the promise of another triumph for Mr. Cleveland's policy.

No sooner had the bill reached the Senate than its prospects became overshadowed.   There it encountered a coalition of vested interests, bent on its destruction;

and as each clause came up for discussion, there was found to be a knot of Democrats ready, on various pretexts of local urgency, to combine with the Republicans.

Before the bill left the Senate, 634 alterations were made, effacing every vestige of its original features. Duties were re-established on raw materials, such as sugar and iron ; and concessions were made to various sections as regards all kinds of manufactured articles. Senators Gorman and Brice had practically taken the bill out of the hands of the party. They, with their Republican allies, proceeded to rearrange it on what they represented as statesmanlike principles of compromise.

As the discussions on the bill proceeded, and it became evident that intrigue had broken up the slender Democratic majority in the Senate, the mortification of the President was extreme. In his message he had earnestly appealed to Congress to subordinate personal desires and ambitions to the general good. "The local interests affected by the proposed reform are," said he, "so numerous, and so varied, that if all are insisted upon the legislation embodying the reform must inevitably fail." When the bill was about to be referred to a Conference of the two Houses, he made one more attempt to recall his followers to a sense of responsibility, and, on the 2nd July, addressed to Mr. Wilson a remarkable letter, which was subsequently read to the House.

"My public life has been so closely related to the subject, I have so longed for its accomplishment, and I have so often promised its realization to my fellow countrymen as a result of their trust and confidence in the

Democratic party, that I hope no excuse is necessary for my earnest appeal to you that in this crisis you strenuously insist upon party honesty, and good faith, and a sturdy adherence to Democratic principles.

"I believe these are absolutely necessary conditions to the continuation of Democratic existence. I cannot rid myself of the feeling that this Conference will present the best, if not the only hope of true Democracy. Indications point to its action as the reliance of those who desire the genuine fruition of Democratic effort, the fulfilment of Democratic pledges, and the redemption of Democratic promises to the people. To reconcile differences in the details comprised within the fixed and well-defined lines of principle, will not be the sole task of the Conference; but, as it seems to me, its members will also have in charge the question whether Democratic principles themselves are to be saved or abandoned.

"There is no excuse for mistaking or misapprehending the feeling and temper of the rank and file of the Democracy. They are downcast under the assertion that their party fails in ability to manage the government, and they are apprehensive that efforts to bring about tariff reform may fail; but they are much more downcast and apprehensive in their fear that Democratic principles may be surrendered."

Whilst deploring the changes that had been made in the bill, he declared, "our abandonment of the cause, or the principles upon which it rests, means party perfidy, and party dishonour."*

This appeal had no more success than the message. There were many Conferences between the two chambers. Mr. Wilson and his friends were resolute in retaining wool upon the free list, but had to yield as regards coal and iron. At length, about the middle of August, a settlement

* *Congressional Record*, vol. 26, p. 7712.

was arrived at, and the bill as amended passed through both Houses. There was an average reduction from the rates imposed by the McKinley Act, amounting to eleven per cent., but the duties were retained on all raw materials except wool. The exemption of wool was in fact the only part of the bill which could be pleaded as a compliance with the pledges on which the House and the President had been elected. It was, however, a very important vindication of principle, and excited the wrath of Mr. McKinley's friends. Senator Sherman calls it the "culminating atrocity of the tariff law,"* and his conviction throws a curious light on what is known as the "American system." He says, "Over a million farmers were engaged in wool growing, and the annual production is $125,000,000. It was a great industry, yet it was left solitary and alone, without the slightest protection given to it, directly or indirectly." The old theory of Protection was, that duties should be levied to foster infant enterprises, but according to Senator Sherman, the larger and more flourishing the industry, the stronger is its claim for sheltering legislation.

When the bill was sent to the President, the Republicans expressed confident hopes that in his disappointment he would exercise his veto. Such a course, however, his friends pointed out, would only prolong the general uncertainty from which business had been suffering since 1890. Defective as the new scheme was, it contained what promised to be important provisions for the relief of the Treasury. The income tax alone was expected to produce a revenue of $30,000,000, which would be security against future deficits.

* SHERMAN, *Recollections*, p. 1205.

It was impossible for Mr. Cleveland to accept the tariff portion of the bill as a discharge of the pledges which he and the party had given. Fortunately the Constitution, on this occasion, supplied a means of turning the labour of Congress to some account, without obscuring the position which the leader of the Democratic party had taken up. He did not veto or sign the bill, but left it without reply for ten days, when it became law on the responsibility of the two Houses. A certain amount of work had been done, but at great cost of time and party credit. The faith of the public in the regenerative influence which Mr. Cleveland's teaching might exercise on general politics, and the Democratic party in particular, was thoroughly shaken. The younger men of the party, it is true, had stood by him consistently in the House of Representatives, but the Senate had been more reckless of its reputation even than in the debates of the previous autumn on the Silver Bill.

A letter, published in the newspapers, showed the mortification which Mr. Cleveland felt at this result of the struggle :—

"I take my place with the rank and file of the Democratic party, who believe in tariff reform, and well know what it is ; who refuse to accept the results embodied in this bill as the close of the war ; who are not blinded to the fact that the livery of Democratic Tariff Reform has been stolen, and worn in the service of Republican Protection ; and who have marked the places where the deadly blight of treason has blasted the councils of the brave in their hour of might. The trusts and combinations — the communism of pelf — whose machinations have prevented us from reaching the success we deserved, should not be forgotten nor forgiven."

Meanwhile, events of a distressing character, outside the ordinary range of politics, were occurring in many parts of the Union. The check to business, the decline in agricultural prices, had stopped employment. Severe individual suffering prevailed in many States, and various popular organizations seized the opportunity to press Socialist schemes upon the attention of the people. There were numerous strikes in the great manufacturing centres. The followers of a Labour leader named Coxey joined in a march to Washington from the Pacific States, and the "Coxeyite army" occasioned some anxiety to the various authorities through whose districts they passed. Much more serious, however, was the conflict with the American Railway Union at Chicago. The Pullman Car Company were involved in a dispute with their employees, and the latter struck work. Their places were filled by others. Then the Union of railway men, on the advice of their President, Debs, took up the question, and demanded that the Railways should boycott the Pullman Company. When this edict was not complied with, they not only struck work themselves, but stopped the working of the lines by other persons. The Governor of Illinois, Mr. Altgeld, had already attracted attention by pardoning some of the persons who were undergoing imprisonment for the Anarchist outrages in 1880. He refused to take the necessary measures to enable the companies to carry on their business. The postmasters in Chicago, who are Federal officers, appealed to Washington for help to distribute the mails, and

Mr. Cleveland at once sent troops to Chicago, when the strike collapsed. In the case of several similar conflicts elsewhere, the troops of the United States had been called in during the summer, but in each of these instances they entered the State at the request of the Governor. To Chicago, however, they were sent not only without that officer's consent, but against his protest. This despatch of an armed force would have involved a serious constitutional question in the former state of the law; but acts passed since 1860 enable the President to send troops into any State where he has reason to believe that Federal business is not adequately protected, or that the lives or property of American citizens are exposed to danger which the local authorities fail to avert.

As this unfortunate year drew to a close, the general disappointment deepened. It was plain that the Democratic party had not risen to the level of intelligence and patriotism maintained by their leader; and chagrin on this account was not mitigated by any change for the better in business, or in the prospects of the Treasury. The deficit at the end of the fiscal year, in June, was much larger than Mr. Carlisle had anticipated, although sixteen millions had been saved on the estimates of public expenditure. There was a decline of over eighty-seven million dollars in the yield of Customs and inland revenue. There were other anxieties besides the provision of funds for the ordinary expenses of government. No effectual remedy had been provided for the disorder of the currency. The legislation of 1893 had put an end to the process of inflation resulting from the Sherman Act; but no progress had been made with the scheme which Mr. Carlisle presented, in the second session, for reducing the enormous existing mass of paper money previously issued, and providing an adequate reserve. The decline in business made the inflation more conspicuous, and stimulated the export of gold ; whilst this very condition of bad times revived the popular cry for more currency, and awakened the hopes of the owners of silver.

Twice this year the slender reserve of gold was threatened, and the President was obliged to make use of the powers given under the Resumption Acts. He bought gold by issuing $50,000,000 worth of five per cent. bonds, to run for ten years. Thus, after all the boasts of national progress, all the exultation at the ease and rapidity with which the war debt had been reduced, the country was again running into debt—and in time of peace. Bad trade, deficits at the Treasury, and additions to the National Debt, were startling results, for which the busy citizen was too much disposed to hold the Government of the day responsible. Republican writers threw all the blame on the tariff reformers, suppressing the fact that the shrinkage in revenue occurred when the McKinley Act was still in force. Their argument is, of course, that the fear of change which arose after the Democratic victory of 1890 deprived McKinley of any fair chance. This may be worth noting as a speculation about what might have been, but it does not justify the general vaunt, that President Harrison's career was marked by surpluses, and President Cleveland's by deficits. The blunder of the McKinley Bill left a long trail of mischief, and the disorders in the currency are of still older origin.

Before there was time to consider these things in their due proportion, the political clock marked the hour for the election of the fifty-fourth Congress, and the Democratic majority of the Cleveland Congress disappeared. In a somewhat larger House the party went down from the two hundred and nineteen seats they held in 1892 to one hundred and four, whilst in the Senate they were in a minority of four, without counting the Populists—six in number on either side.

It was in such depressing circumstances that the final session of the fifty-third Congress opened in December, 1894. The urgent work was the adjustment of the currency, but this was a task which a party who had recently sustained a damaging defeat were not in a position to accomplish.

The annual message was less controversial than usual. It was only when treating of the subject of pensions, of which the amount in 1895 was estimated at $140,000,000, that Mr. Cleveland deigned to notice the attacks of his adversaries. He mentioned the fact that extensive frauds had been discovered, and went on :

" The accusation that an effort to detect pension frauds is evidence of unfriendliness towards our worthy veterans, and a denial of their claims to the generosity of the Government, suggests an unfortunate indifference to the commission of any offence which has for its motive the securing of a pension, and indicates a willingness to be blind to the existence of mean and treacherous crimes which play upon demagogic fears and make sport of the patriotic impulse of a grateful people."*

He reminded Congress that he was still without any

---

* *Annual Message*, December, 1894, p. 26.

means of maintaining the equality between gold and silver except by using the power of issuing bonds; there were theories abroad against the use of this power, but convinced as he was that the adoption of a silver standard would be a public calamity, he was resolved to employ the powers of borrowing, in the act of 1875, "whenever, and as often as it becomes necessary to maintain a sufficient gold reserve, and in abundant time to save the credit of our country, and make good the financial declarations of our Government."

This defiance of the advocates of silver did not secure him any help from Congress. The demoralization of the majority, which had already begun in the previous spring, had become worse since the disasters at the ballot boxes in November, 1894; and the President's request received no more attention than his warnings against the operation of the Bland Act, in his first administration. With the new year the exports of gold began again. In February the gold reserve had fallen to $41,000,000, and Mr. Cleveland once more addressed Congress, asking for power to issue three per cent. bonds, to be repaid in gold, not in coin. These gold bonds he would have been able to sell readily, but a bill for this object was rejected by a majority of forty-four, and he had no resource except to return to the system authorized by the Resumption Acts. He issued $62,000,000 four per cent. bonds, to be redeemed in coin, and to run for thirty years, a transaction which involved an expenditure of sixteen millions of dollars more than that proposed by the President; and this loss was incurred because the majority of Congress refused to hurt the feelings of the silver party by using

N

the word gold. The passage of any such bill as the President advised would have been almost sufficient in itself to have checked the public apprehension, and gold would have flowed back to the country through the ordinary channels of commerce.

The troubles of the Treasury did not end with this new loan. Several appeals to the Law Courts had been made against the legality of the income tax, and in June, 1895, a test case was brought before the Supreme Court. That tribunal decided, by a majority of one, that the tax, as imposed by the act, was unconstitutional, and that the money already levied under it must be refunded. Thus the Treasury lost a source of revenue expected to yield $30,000,000, and the chance of avoiding a deficit disappeared. The only consoling circumstance was that the new tariff had begun to work favourably, and there was an increase of over $20,000,000 from Customs.

When the fifty-fourth Congress opened in December, 1895, the drain of gold had begun again: the reserve had fallen to $79,000,000. After the usual review of foreign relations, he devoted the remainder of a long message to currency, recounting the unfortunate variations in policy since the passing of the Resumption Act, the reckless additions to the monetary circulation, and the expense entailed by the efforts to keep up the reserve. The Government had paid in gold more than nine-tenths of its notes; but as they had all been paid out again, it owed them still. It had paid gold for half of the notes issued under the Silver Purchase Bill; but they, too, had been paid out again, and not extinguished. To carry on this system, a sum of $257,815,000 had been added to the National Debt, involving an annual charge of $11,000,000.

The only practicable remedy, he declared, would be found in the retirement and cancellation of the green-backs and the Treasury coin notes, and this might be readily accomplished by the exchange of these notes for United States bonds of various denominations, bearing a low rate of interest. Were the currency re-organized in this way, use might ultimately be made of the hoards of silver in the Treasury vaults. He also urged such alterations of the laws on banking as would bring banking facilities "near to the people in all sections of the country."

This message is a document which bears comparison with the famous tariff message of 1887. It is a complete and exhaustive treatise on the condition of the currency, and fearlessly exposes the unscrupulousness of the owners of silver, and the folly of the inflationist party. When we consider that it was sent to a Congress specially chosen to prepare the way for the return to power of his political opponents, it is an interesting record of his enduring faith in the common sense of the nation. Mr. Cleveland has always acted on the rule that the people were capable of understanding the truth, if it was clearly and frankly put before them. He could not have expected much aid from the men he was addressing; but he recollected that the message of 1887, slight as was the impression it made on the fiftieth Congress, produced ultimately signal results throughout the country. The final session of the preceding Congress had closed with a great display of activity among the friends of silver. In the preparations for the coming Presidential Election, the advocates of free coinage had been showing their strength, both in the Republican and the Democratic camp.

The evils he pointed out were left without remedy, and new financial difficulties arose ; but before concluding the account of his administration up to the autumn of 1896, some space must be given to a new line of policy adopted in December last, which he announced shortly after the opening of the new Congress. On Tuesday, the 17th December, he sent a message to Congress which not only aroused keen interest throughout the Union, but made him famous in countries where American Presidents had rarely been heard of. Up to this time, he was known as the fearless champion of law and public integrity. Acts of Congress were not to him advertisements of particular opinions, but assertions of principle binding on the community. He insisted that they should be definite and practical, and should be faithfully administered. Schemes for the aggrandizement of individuals, or of localities, at the expense of the public, he resisted, absolutely indifferent whether they came from one party or the other. He had been hitherto known to his countrymen as the inexorable enemy of the political jobber. Suddenly he appeared before the world on this Tuesday evening as the founder of a new foreign policy.

CHAPTER XIII.

FOREIGN RELATIONS OF THE UNITED STATES.

Washington's injunction — **Popular desire for** a foreign policy—
American diplomatists—The Keiley dispute—Hawaiian Revolution
— **Mr. Cleveland** withdraws Annexation Treaty — The Blount
inquiry — Public sentiment **as to** "Monarchic Government"—
Senator Morgan—Cuba.

THE struggle made by Mr. Cleveland to promote
financial and fiscal reforms; the unflinching spirit
in which he endeavoured to apply the old principles of
Democratic policy to the complex life of the vast community which has grown up within the last sixty years,
seem topics sufficient to fill this small volume. The
Venezuela Message, however, has attracted so much
attention to the foreign relations of the Union, that it
is necessary to give some account of this side of
American policy. Washington's famous injunction to
avoid entangling alliances with other Powers has been
hitherto regarded as the Alpha and Omega of the
external policy of the Republic, and to this celebrated
utterance Mr. Cleveland has more than once appealed.
As the country grew in wealth and population, there
gradually sprang up a widespread desire that American
citizens should have their part in those excitements

which, owing to hereditary animosities, to frontier disputes, to intersecting waves of population, and limited territory, the older nations enjoy in great abundance. This feeling is active among the great multitude of well-to-do Americans who travel in Europe and other parts of the world, and are not content that their country should be without a share of the interests which occupy the minds of Europeans. The existence of such tendencies encourages some study of international relations : and accordingly, for many years past, a large portion of the time of Congress, particularly in the Senate, has been given up to discussions upon the affairs of other nations. This habit is agreeable to the self-esteem of the Senators. It is an opportunity for flights of eloquence ; it compromises no one, and suggests a number of topics to the local orators throughout the country. Disquisitions on foreign affairs are exceedingly vague, and generally without any distinct aim or political result. These themes are to ambitious statesmen much what certain classes of securities on the Stock Exchange are to the frequenters of that institution, counters to play with when serious business is not on hand. They amuse the outside public, and may sometimes bring an increase of fame and influence.

Closely connected with this inclination to look at foreign questions from their bearing on the future of individual statesmen, or the chances of securing votes at some election, is the unwillingness to recognize diplomacy as a regular profession. The United States is the only nation—I do not say of the first rank, but of any international position—which thinks it possible to dispense with a long course of training for the men who may be charged to conduct correspondence with foreign countries. They vaunt that, as a plain people, the Americans are able to dispense with any service of the kind. Accordingly their Ambassadors and Ministers to Europe are generally retired politicians, with now and again an eminent man of letters. None of them retain their positions long enough to exercise much influence on the relations between European Governments and Washington. There are occasionally notable exceptions — men who have made a special study of European affairs, and whose tact and knowledge inspire confidence, and secure them authority with the governments to which they are accredited. Mr. Charles Francis Adams, at the Court of St. James', Mr. Motley, serving his successive appointments in Germany and Austria, and, in later years, General Meredith Reade, in Athens, are instances of this exceptional class which will at once occur to the mind of the reader. But the prevailing rule is that the Ambassador or Minister is appointed because it suits his convenience or the convenience of the Government that he should find employment abroad, rather than because he possesses any special qualifications for the work.

A curious example of the mode in which these posts are filled occurred in Mr. Cleveland's first year of office. Mr. Keiley was nominated ambassador to Rome, and was about to undertake the duties, when the Italian Government reminded Mr. Bayard that the new ambassador had become notorious in previous years, owing to an unmeasured attack upon the personal character

of King Victor Emmanuel. King Humbert declined
to receive at his Court the popular assailant of his
father. This objection was, of course, insuperable, and
Mr. Bayard consoled himself with the idea that the
difficulty might be solved by sending the orator to
Vienna. Perhaps it was fondly imagined that the
animosity of the American diplomatist towards the
destroyers of the Temporal Power would evoke a sym-
pathetic welcome from Austrian society. Count Kalnoky,
however, objected to receiving an envoy whose presence
had been found impossible at the Court of the Emperor
of Austria's neighbour and ally. In the course of subsequent semi-official communications, it was incidentally
remarked that Mr. Keiley had married a lady of the
Hebrew race. This circumstance, it was suggested,
might entail social difficulties, in the then state of
opinion at Vienna, and make it more agreeable for Mr.
Keiley to find a sphere for his abilities elsewhere. The
fact was mentioned, rather as one for the consideration
of the envoy than as a ground of objection ; but the
observation was immediately taken advantage of to send
Count Kalnoky a lecture on the American Constitution.

Austria was reminded that the Republic is "a
government of laws, that religious liberty is the chief
corner-stone of the American system of government." *
"The self-respect of a nation of sixty millions of free
men" was invoked. In reply to this eloquence, Count
Kalnoky remarked, "We do not want Mr. Keiley, and
ought we not to be judges for ourselves ? "

An Ambassador, according to European notions, is a

* *House Ex. Docs.* 1885-86, vol. i. p. 40.

foreigner admitted to close relations with the Government in order that his own country may have the benefit of his information and his services, as a friendly intermediary on the spot, whenever any controversy arises. That he should be a person with whom the Government to which he is accredited, and the people about that Government, would be likely to get on, is an essential condition of his being able to do the work for which he is employed. This was not the aspect in which the matter was regarded by the Secretary of State. To Mr. Bayard, Mr. Keiley was an American citizen, appointed by the President of Senate to a post of $10,000 a year; and interference by crowned heads in the choice of officers of the Republic was not to be tolerated.

Not only was America for some time without any Minister at Vienna, but both the President and his Secretary recorded the incident as evidence to their countrymen of their public spirit. The objections made to an "estimable citizen" were such, Mr. Cleveland declared, as "could not be acquiesced in without violation of my oath of office, and the precepts of the Constitution." In a popular history of Mr. Cleveland, the controversy is thus referred to:

"The letters which Mr. Bayard wrote in defence of this policy have seldom been excelled in our diplomatic literature for careful writing, sound views, and loftiness of thought. The President, in his first annual message, announced the policy he had adopted, and added a spirited rebuke to that administered by his Secretary." *

By people who talk in this way, the foreign department, it

* PARKER'S *Cleveland*, 1892, p. 168.

is evident, is regarded only as an opportunity for showing their fine metal towards countries less enlightened than themselves, and such opportunities are the more eagerly seized if the foreign government happens to be a monarchy.

It is only fair to Mr. Cleveland to say that with this popular mode of treating other nations he has not evinced much sympathy. He has several times shown in his dealings with other governments a true sense of justice and dignity. That the light in which these questions generally present themselves to him is very different from that prevailing in the Foreign Affairs Committee of the Senate, is conspicuous in the cases of Hawaii and of Cuba.

One of the first duties imposed upon his Cabinet in 1893, was to come to a decision on the plan for the annexation of the Sandwich Islands. Although Mr. Cleveland had been elected President in November, and was to assume office on the 4th March, General Harrison, and the Secretary of State, Mr. Forster, had settled a treaty for annexation in the earlier part of February. It was sent to the Senate for ratification on the 15th of that month. A proposal to establish the sovereignty of the Union over territory 2000 miles away from the American continent was in itself so novel, that it might well have made the new administration pause; but there were many other circumstances connected with this project which suggested caution. Mr. Cleveland promptly informed the Senate that the Executive withdrew the treaty until there was time to consider the whole subject. The Hon. James H. Blount, of Georgia, a gentleman of high position and experience in public affairs, was sent by the President as special commissioner to Hawaii. His report disclosed a singular story of violence, and unscrupulous abuse of the privileges of international law.

These islands are the most northern of the groups scattered over the Pacific, and possess a population of some 90,000, of which about half is of native blood, the original race being of the Maori type. Lying nearer to the United States than any other considerable cluster in the Pacific, they early attracted the attention of that Republic. The United States was the first Power to recognize the independence of the islands. Everett, in 1843, said :

"The course adopted by this Government, in regard to the Sandwich Islands, has for its sole object the preservation of the independence of those islands, and the maintenance by their Government of an entire partiality in their intercourse with foreign states."

There is a prosperous white population, numbering some 6000, born in the island, mostly of American descent. From them, for some years past, the Government and chief public officials have been appointed ; but many of the people most active in administration were native-born Americans, who had not renounced their American citizenship.

In 1887 a new Constitution was established, and this admitted every male resident to vote, without being called on to renounce allegiance to the country of his birth. One result was to throw the management of affairs almost entirely into the hands of the Americans, whilst a continual agitation went on among the natives for a return to the old state of things. King Kalukaua died in 1891, and Queen Liliuokalani succeeded to the throne. During the next two years, the foreign officials appear to have matured their plans for abandoning any pretence of native government.

The obligation of the envoys of a foreign State to abstain from any interference in the politics of the country to which they are commissioned, is a common-place of all text-books on international law; but as early as February, 1892, the American Minister at Honolulu, Mr. John L. Stevens, wrote to his Government in the following terms:

"There are increasing indications that the annexation sentiment is gaining among the business men, as well as with the less responsible of the foreign and native population of the islands. . . . The intelligent and responsible men here, unaided by outside support, are too few in number to control in political affairs, and to secure good government. . . . At a future time . . . I shall deem it my official duty to give a more elaborate statement of facts and reasons why a new departure by the United States as to Hawaii is rapidly becoming a necessity, that a protectorate is impracticable, and that annexation must be the future remedy, else Great Britain will be furnished with circumstances and opportunity to get a hold on these islands, which will cause future serious embarrassment to the United States."

Mr. Stallings, of Alabama, speaking in Congress, said:

"The correspondence of Mr. Stevens clearly shows that, early in his administration, he formed designs of annexing these islands to the United States. It appears to have been his dream by night, and the constant companion of his thoughts by day. The whole energy of his being was devoted to this plan; and it is clearly deducible from the evidence, that the State Department at Washington was not averse to lending a willing ear to his seductive scheme."

During the next month he wrote to Mr. Blaine, asking for special instructions,

"in case the Government here should be reorganized and overturned by an orderly and peaceful revolutionary movement, largely of native Hawaiians, and a Provisional or Republican Government organized and proclaimed. ...

"I have information, which I deem reliable, that there is an organized revolutionary party in the islands, composed largely of native Hawaiians, and a considerable number of whites and half-whites, led chiefly by individuals of the latter two classes.

"These people," he goes on, "are very likely to overthrow the monarchy and establish a republic, with the ultimate view of annexation to the United States. I may add that the annexation sentiment is increasing quite as much among the white residents and Hawaiians, and other working men who own no sugar stock, as with the sugar planters."

This despatch of the 8th March shows that Mr. Stevens was in the confidence of the conspirators. With the exception of his statement as to the proportion of natives in the revolutionary party, these letters supply almost a record of what actually occurred the January following.

Towards the end of the year 1892, Admiral Skerritt, who was about to assume command of the Pacific Squadron of the United States, called at the Navy Department for final instructions, December 30th, and in the course of the interview said:

"Mr. Tracy, I want to ask you about these Hawaiian affairs. When I was out there, twenty years ago, I had frequent conversations with the then United States Minister, Mr. Pierce, on the subject of the islands. I was told then that the United States Government did not wish to annex the islands of Hawaii."

He replied, "Commodore, the wishes of the Government have changed, they will be very glad to annex Hawaii." He said, "As a matter of course, none but the ordinary legal means can be used to persuade these people to come into the United States."

"I said, 'All right, sir, I only wanted to know how things were going on as a cue to my action,' and I bade him good-bye." *

Admiral Skerritt did not proceed immediately to Honolulu; but in the harbour there was a vessel belonging to the Pacific Squadron, the *Boston*, under the command of Captain Wiltze.

On Saturday, January 14th, 1893, Parliament was opened by the Queen. There were many rumours that she intended to promulgate a new Constitution, and that two, at least, of her Ministers were in favour of the project. After the formal ceremonies, and before the Queen met her Cabinet, the foreign envoys sought an interview with the Ministers, and Mr. Wodehouse, the English Minister, mentioned the prevailing reports, and asked for information. Mr. Parker, on behalf of the Cabinet, said that he and his colleagues had determined to advise the Queen against the proposed change. The Cabinet, in their subsequent account to Mr. Blount, gave a curious picture of Mr. Stevens' disappointment at the prospect of losing the desired opportunity for intervention.

"This reply was satisfactory to all the representatives except to Mr. Stevens, the American Minister, who became excited, and, dropping the subject under discussion, pounded his cane upon the floor, and stated, in a loud voice, that the United States had been insulted, and that the passage of the Lottery Bill was a direct

* *Report on Hawaii*, 1893, p. 10.

attack **upon** his Government. The other representatives tried to **change the** subject, **and, finally** succeeding, the meeting broke up after several **of them had** disclaimed any approbation of Mr. Stevens' remarks." *

The Cabinet then waited **upon the Queen, and she** consented, after some hesitation, to give up her plan of abolishing the existing Constitution. This resolution was announced to the people assembled in the palace, and all **danger of** trouble seemed **at an end.** When, however, the Ministers met on Sunday, they were told that a "Committee of Safety" had been formed the night before, with the cognizance of Mr. Stevens. Popular meetings had been called, one by the agitators, another by the Queen's friends, for Monday, to discuss the situation; and early that morning the Queen issued a proclamation, disclaiming any intention to seek alterations except by the methods provided in the existing Constitution. Mr. Thurston, the leader of the American party, declined to postpone the meeting which he and his friends had called.

About half-past two, whilst these meetings were being held, Mr. Stevens went on board the *Boston*, and left Captain Wiltze a request to land marines and sailors, in view of the existing critical circumstances. Everything on board had been made ready for the landing. At the meeting of the Queen's friends, motions were passed thanking her for the proclamation; whilst the other assembly, held in a different part of the town, charged the "Committee of Safety" to devise means to secure the permanent maintenance of law and order. The

* *Report on Hawaii,* p. 81.

meeting separated quietly, and the Committee wrote to Mr. Stevens, declaring that general alarm and terror prevailed, and asking for the protection of the United States forces.

At this time the town was in enjoyment of peace; no disturbance was apparent anywhere, and the legal Government had undisputed control over 500 armed men and several pieces of artillery. Mr. Blount tells us that whilst these conferences were going on, "the great body of the people moved in their accustomed course. Women and children passed to and fro through the streets seemingly unconscious of any impending danger." There is no record of any formal answer to the letter of the Committee; but at five o'clock the marines were landed with two Gatling guns and were marched—not to the United States Consulate, which would have been their natural goal if there were any real danger to American citizens—but to a public hall within 150 yards of the Palace and close to the public offices. The Royal Governor of the Island, and Mr. Parker, the Minister of Foreign Affairs, addressed a protest to Mr. Stevens. In the afternoon of Tuesday, the "Committee of Public Safety," with two or three friends, appeared on the steps of the public offices, where the American troops were assembled, and proclaimed the abolition of the Monarchy and the institution of a Provisional Government, "to exist until terms of union with the United States of America have been negotiated and agreed upon." The new Government, of which Mr. Dole was the head, was at once recognized by Mr. Stevens. A gentleman, who was not a party to the conspiracy, was sent to the Queen to point out the danger of a conflict with the forces of the United States. He urged her to submit under protest, and appeal to Washington.

The Queen adopted this advice, issued a protest, and sent formal letters of appeal addressed both to General Harrison and to Mr. Cleveland. Martial law was proclaimed in the city, and, as there were now signs of disorder among the forces collected by the new Government, Commander Wiltze, on the 1st February, took possession of the islands on behalf of the United States. Meanwhile the treaty of annexation was drafted at Washington by the agents of President Dole and Mr. Forster, who had succeeded Mr. Blaine as Secretary of State.

Mr. Blount arrived at Honolulu on the 26th March, and having satisfied himself that no disorder would arise from his putting an end to the anomalous position held by the United States forces, he directed that the flag should be hauled down on the 1st April, and the men re-embarked. He then proceeded to collect full details as to the transactions of January.

When Mr. Blount completed his report, towards the end of the summer, Mr. Gresham, in a lucid State paper, advised the President that the project of annexation ought not to be entertained ; and, he added, "should not the great wrong done to a feeble but independent State, by an abuse of this authority of the United States, be undone by restoring the legitimate Government?"

This line the President adopted in his annual message of December, 1893. After reviewing the facts disclosed, he declared :

"Our duty does not, in my opinion, end with refusing to consummate this questionable transaction. . . . . By an act of war committed with the participation of a diplomatic representative of the United States, and without authority of Congress, the Government of a feeble but friendly and confiding people has been overthrown. . . . . The Provisional Government has not assumed a republican or other constitutional form, but has remained a mere executive council, or oligarchy, set up without the assent of the people. It has not sought to find a permanent basis of popular support, and has given no evidence of any intention to do so."

As to the revolution, he says :

"The President is satisfied that the movement against the Queen, if not instigated, was encouraged and supported by the representative of this Government at Honolulu; that he promised in advance to aid her enemies in an effort to overthrow the Hawaiian Government, and set up by force a new Government in its place, and that he kept this promise by causing a detachment of troops to be landed from the *Boston*, on the 16th January, and by recognizing the Provisional Government the next day, when it was too feeble to defend itself, and the Constitutional Government was able to successfully maintain its authority against any threatening force other than that of the United States already landed. The Queen," he adds, "surrendered, not to the Provisional Government, but to the United States ; she surrendered, not absolutely and permanently, but conditionally, until such time as the facts could be considered by the United States"; and he urges that in case an amnesty were obtained for the men who were encouraged by the officers of the United States, "the restored Government should resume its authority as if its continuity had never been interrupted."*

President Dole, however, and Vice-President Damon were not to be coaxed into any surrender of their position. They postponed giving any answer to the proposals of

* *Report on Hawaii,* p. xxii.

Mr. Willis, who had been sent in place of Mr. Stevens, until July 4th, 1894, when they proclaimed a new Constitution of the Republic of Hawaii, declaring Mr. Dole President until December, 1900. There is abundant evidence that this step had as little general support as the declaration of January 17th, 1893 ; but in the interval the conspirators had secured possession of public funds, and organized a considerable contingent of troops from among the lower classes of the foreign immigrants. The United States Senate passed a resolution in favour of the recognition of the new Republic. This practically took the question out of Mr. Cleveland's hands. Once President Dole and his eighteen friends were recognized as an existing Government, it was impossible for the President to employ the forces of the United States against the Hawaiian army of mercenaries without the authority of Congress. For the subsequent events in the islands the reader is referred to Mr. Julius Palmer's pathetic account of its condition under President Dole.* More important than the fate of these islands is the curious light which the discussion of this subject throws on the attitude of Congress, and especially upon the opinions current in the Senate.

The spirit which Mr. Cleveland's message evoked in Congress is shown in the following motions :—

Mr. Hitt, of Illinois, proposed :

"That it is the sense of this House that the demand caused by the President of the United States, by his imperative instructions, to be made on December 19th last, upon the President and officers of the Hawaiian Government, that it promptly relinquish all authority, and

* *Again in Hawaii.* By JULIUS A. PALMER. Boston, 1895.

his proposed erection of a monarchy in its stead, was an unwarranted intervention in the affairs of a friendly recognized Government, contrary to the law of nations, the policy and traditions of this Republic, and the spirit of the Constitution." *

Mr. Blair, of New Hampshire, endeavoured to preclude the President from any attempt to restore the Queen, by the following motion :

"That the Provisional Government of Hawaii having been duly recognized, the highest international interests require that it shall pursue its own line of polity ; and foreign intervention in the political affairs of these islands will be regarded as an act unfriendly to the Government of the United States."

The fact that Mr. Cleveland was actually assisting to restore a monarchy was made the more odious by repeated attacks upon the unfortunate Queen who had been so scandalously deprived of her crown. Of these calumnies Mr. Blount says :

"Their frequent repetition in Mr. Stevens' correspondence with the State Department, caused him to make some enquiry into the subject."

And after expressing his belief that they are without foundation, he adds :

. . . . "Evidently this charge against the Queen has for its foundation the looseness which comes from passionate and vindictive partisan struggles in Honolulu."†

By the end of February, 1894, the Foreign Relations Committee, presided over by Mr. Morgan, a Democratic Senator from Alabama, brought up a report which was intended as a vindication of Mr. Stevens, and a lecture

* *Congressional Record*, vol. **26**, p. **1814.**
† *Ibid.* p. 68.

to the President on the "condition of public sentiment as to 'Monarchic Government.'"*

"In the Western Hemisphere, except as to the colonial relation which has become one of mere political alliance, chiefly for commercial reasons, and does not imply in any notable case absolute subjection to Imperial or Royal authority, royalty no longer exists. When a crown falls in any kingdom of the Western Hemisphere, it is pulverised; when a sceptre departs, it departs for ever: and American opinion cannot sustain any American ruler in the attempt to restore them, no matter how virtuous and sincere the reasons may be that seem to justify him."

Any attack upon royalty is, in its nature, Mr. Morgan argues, an endeavour to vindicate natural right, and such "efforts of men to recover their natural rights of self-government should not be narrowly questioned. The presumption of law should be favourable, rather than unfriendly, to such movements for the establishment by the people of the foundation of their liberties, based upon their right to govern themselves." †

"'This doctrine,'" it is added, "'is modern in England, where the right to the crown and its prerogatives have (*sic*) bled the people for fifteen centuries.'" As England had absolutely refrained from any interference in the Hawaiian controversy, it is not easy to see why this glimpse of English history was added for the instruction of the Senate; but it illustrates the tendency of public men at the other side of the Atlantic to decry England without reference to the question in hand.

The Committee on Foreign Relations is practically the machinery for the exercise of the powers confided to the

---

* *Congressional Record*, vol. 26, p. 2414.
† *Ibid.* p. 2415.

Senate by the Constitution in regard to Foreign States. It has attributes which give it much higher authority than any other Committee of Congress. In this department of business the Senate eclipses the President and the Supreme Court, and the reports of its committees cannot be treated as mere party manifestoes. It is true, as we have seen in the case of Cuba, that the Committee cannot compel the President to act upon their opinions, no more than he can compel them to confirm any treaty he may make ; but their reports are the formal exposition of public policy, by the highest authority on foreign affairs known to the American people, and we see that according to these teachers the ordinary amity between Governments is qualified by the consideration whether the foreign State is a Monarchy or a Republic. If the foreign Government comes under the former category, its rights are liable to be interpreted according to a special set of principles. A Monarchy is, in fact, somewhat in the position occupied by the Christian States in any negotiations with the Moslem statesmen of former days. Faith might be kept with them, powers might be conceded to them ; but all this depended very much on the sense of expediency or the magnanimity of the followers of the Prophet. They were outside the political world which Islam recognized.

No one can doubt that the views expressed by Mr. Morgan represent the prevailing current of opinion in the Union, from the days of Calhoun to the present time. If a Senator now and then indulges in homage to better principles, he takes care before long to make up for these eccentricities by some extravagant tribute to national folly. Foreign topics are for the most part regarded in Congress as means of securing some surplus political capital for men whose political fortunes are staked on burning questions of home policy.

The case of Cuba it is not necessary to examine in any detail. That island is the last remnant of the Spanish Empire in America : a country with great natural resources and spacious harbours, only 130 miles from the coast of Florida. For fifty years past, its relations with the mother country have been unhappy. The rebellious inhabitants have no desire for absorption by the United States. On the other hand, there can be no doubt that the troubles have been fermented by exiles and sympathizers residing within the Union ; and whenever civil war has been raging, aid in men, arms, and money has been sent from American ports. Long is the series of disputes between Spain and the Republic : the former Power complaining that the neutrality laws were not properly enforced ; the United States protesting against the seizure of American vessels, or the arrest of American subjects. There has always been a party in the Union who cast covetous eyes on this island, but few people are prepared to see its population enrolled among American citizens ; whilst to govern it as a dependency would involve new principles of policy at variance with the spirit of American institutions.

The rebellion which is still raging broke out in the early part of 1895. Mr. Cleveland took immediate steps to enforce the neutrality laws, and war vessels were despatched to prevent filibustering expeditions from the coast of Florida. In the annual message last December,

he appealed to his countrymen to fulfil the obligations
of international law.

"The plain duty of their Government is to observe
in good faith the recognized obligations of international
relationship. The performance of this duty should not
be made more difficult by a disregard on the part of our
citizens of the obligations growing out of their allegiance
to their country, which should restrain them from violating,
as individuals, the neutrality which the nation, of which
they are members, is bound to observe in its relations to
friendly sovereign States." *

His good faith in this respect has been recognized by
the Spanish authorities.   As the struggle went on, the
Cuban sympathizers became more noisy in the Atlantic
cities ; and since the fifty-fourth Congress opened, and
the Presidential season began, there has been fierce competition among the leaders of both parties as to which
should carry off the palm for violence towards Spain.
Sometimes the honours were with Senator Lodge ; again
the star of Senator Morgan was in the ascendant ; and
finally Senator Sherman distanced all competitors.

In April a resolution was passed by both Houses in
favour of recognizing the insurgents as belligerents.   The
only attention which the President has bestowed upon
the labours of the Senate was to repeat in July, in still
more explicit terms, the proclamation of neutrality which
he had issued in 1895.

* *President's Message*, 1895, p. 13.

CHAPTER XIV.

AMERICA AND GREAT BRITAIN.

Important relations between the two countries—South American trade—British Guiana—Old dispute with Venezuela—The Olney Despatch—Lord Salisbury's replies—The Venezuela Message—Enthusiasm in Congress—Panic in Stocks—Finance Message—Feeling towards England—Republican impatience of European influence on the American Continent—The Maine and Oregon boundaries.

TO the general principle that foreign affairs are only a pastime of the American politician, there are two exceptions. One Power there is with whom the United States has continuous relations, whose policy engages close attention throughout the Union: and that is Great Britain. Her commercial system dominates that trading world in which the Union plays a large part. Her flag flies along the whole of the northern frontier. Closely connected with this special position of Great Britain is the group of questions affecting the relative position of the United States and the Spanish Republics. In spite of distance, England is the successful competitor of the American trader among those nations whom political orators claim as the pupils of Republican statesmen. The commercial preponderance which Great Britain enjoys in South America keeps alive among the adventurous classes that dislike of the European State which, on the northern frontier, is aroused by the spectacle of a prosperous, orderly, industrious community of English - speaking people who are not worshippers of Republican ideals. The history of the Fisheries question, told in a previous chapter, shows how persistent this feeling of antagonism is in relation to the Dominion of Canada. The keenness of this jealousy, where other parts of the American continent are concerned, was suddenly exhibited last year by the new complexion given to a long - standing controversy about a remote British possession.

British Guiana is a part of South America lying between the rivers Orinoco and Corentin. The principal river within the territory is the Essequibo, which flows into the Atlantic, nearly due north, from the mountains of Brazil. In its course it is fed by several tributaries, which have their sources in the ranges of the north-west lying between it, the Essequibo, and the watershed of the Orinoco. The principal of these is the Cuyuni. It rises in the south - east, and flows westward until its junction with the Uruan, when it sweeps round in a sharp curve to the east, and flows into the Essequibo. How far the watersheds of these tributaries, and of one .or two smaller rivers like the Barima and the Waini, running directly into the Atlantic, are included within British territory, is the question which has been in dispute for many years.

The settlements along the coast came into English

hands in 1796, as a cession from Holland. Although the Spaniards, for many generations, maintained a sort of Monroe doctrine in relation to the whole continent, the commercial establishments of the Dutch in this region were formally acknowledged by the Treaty of Munster, 1648, which put an end to the long war between Spain and the United Provinces. The Dutch settlements undoubtedly extended along the coast as far as Point Barima, where a river of that name falls into the estuary of the Orinoco ; but the Treaty of Munster not only recognized the right of the Netherlands to all territory of which they were in occupation at the time of the treaty, but also to other land which they might acquire afterwards, without encroaching upon Spain. The Dutch gradually moved up the watersheds to the south and west, and acquired control of the basin of the Cuyuni ; whilst, down to 1723, the only Spanish settlement to the south of the Orinoco was that of St. Thome de la Guayana. During the following ninety years, Capuchin missions, coming from the Orinoco, penetrated this region, and gradually extended their operations southwards and eastwards, in the direction of the Dutch possessions.

In 1810, Venezuela declared her independence of the Crown of Spain.

In 1840, Sir Robert Schomburgk, who had previously visited the country at the request of the Royal Geographical Society, was authorized by the British Government to make a survey of the colony. The Venezuelan Government complained of certain posts erected by him, near the Orinoco. These had been put up as landmarks to aid in the work of surveying, and Lord Aberdeen consented to remove them, declaring, at the same time, that the British Government did not thereby abandon any portion of their rights. In 1842, discussions commenced between Great Britain and Venezuela concerning the boundary. The latter State claimed that the territory of their Republic extended to the Essequibo, on the grounds that the Spaniards had, at an early date, explored the Orinoco, and the adjoining valleys of the Barima and other rivers ; and that, at the time of the Munster Treaty, the Dutch had no possessions in the country to the north-west of the Essequibo.

Lord Aberdeen, in reply, appealed to the history of numerous Dutch settlements along the coast during the sixteenth century, and on the rivers between the Esse-quibo and the Orinoco. In 1850 there was much popular excitement in Venezuela, and rumours of military preparations in England. The Government at Caracas was pressed by Congress to erect forts at certain points on the coast ; and, after some correspondence, it was agreed that neither of the contending parties should attempt any formal occupation of the disputed territory, such as would be implied by the construction of forts, or the establishment of military posts.*

In 1876, when the late Lord Derby was Secretary for Foreign Affairs, the claims of Venezuela were again advanced, on the same basis as thirty-one years before, reliance being furthermore placed upon the Bull of Alexander VI. (1496), as importing "a fresh and most

* *Parl. Papers, Venezuela,* No. 1, 1896, p. 256.

valuable recognition" of the right of Spain to the territory of America.* It was maintained, too, that the
Capuchins had extended their settlements to the sea as
far as Cape Nassau, close to New Amsterdam. There
is no trace of any such occupation in the locality.

Various lines of frontier were discussed between the
two Governments, but without result; and in 1883 the
English Minister pressed for a settlement. Venezuela
replied that the laws of the Republic made mutual concessions impossible, inasmuch as no portion of territory
"assumed to constitute a part of the dominions of the
Republic" could be ceded or exchanged; and they
proposed a reference to arbitration. The British Government pointed out that the very same objection might
apply to the carrying out of the award of arbitrators.
And the negotiations dragged on. In the meantime,
conferences were held for the purpose of arranging a
Treaty of Commerce between the two countries; and
the following Article was proposed by the Venezuelan
Minister, and after some discussion accepted by Lord
Granville, in May 1885 (Art. 15).

"If, as it is to be deprecated, there shall arise between
the United States of Venezuela and the United Kingdom
of Great Britain and Ireland any differences which
cannot be adjusted by the usual means of friendly
negotiation, the two contracting parties agree to submit
the decision of all such differences to the arbitration of a
third Power, or of several Powers in amity with both,
without resorting to war, and that the result of such
arbitration shall be binding upon both Governments.

"The arbitrating Power or Powers shall be selected
by the two Governments by common consent; failing

* Parl. Papers, Venezuela, No. 1, 1896, p. 286.

which each of the parties shall nominate an arbitrating Power, and the arbitrators thus appointed shall be requested to select another Power to act as Umpire.

"The procedure of the arbitration shall in each case be determined by the contracting parties; failing which the arbitrating Power or Powers shall be themselves entitled to determine it beforehand." *

A change of Ministry took place whilst these conferences were proceeding, and Lord Salisbury becoming Minister for Foreign Affairs, pointed out that these provisions were too vague. Difficulties arose upon other clauses, and the Treaty was abandoned.

In 1886 the negotiations were resumed, but without result. Meantime it appeared that the Venezuelan Government were making grants of land for colonization in the valley of the Barima. The British authorities warned settlers that these grants would not be recognized. The Venezuelan Government announced their intention to erect a lighthouse on Point Barima. They ultimately claimed the whole watershed of the river Barima, and required its immediate evacuation by England, and the submission of the whole question of frontier to arbitration. As these demands were not complied with, diplomatic relations were suspended by Venezuela in March, 1887.

The negotiations which the Venezuelan Government initiated in 1890 and 1893 for the renewal of diplomatic relations and settlement of boundary dispute, were doomed to failure as long as Venezuela insisted that in any scheme of arbitration which the two countries

---

* *Parl. Papers, Venezuela,* No. 1, p. 308.

might agree on, the whole of the territory between the Essequibo and the Orinoco should be included.

Although it was matter of common knowledge that this controversy existed, it had not in recent years attracted much attention outside Venezuela. In his first Presidency, Mr. Cleveland had encountered considerable difficulty in exacting compensation from that Republic for injuries done to Americans some twenty years before. These claims were frequently alluded to in the messages, and owing to changes of Government at Caracas, were not disposed of when Mr. Cleveland resumed office in 1893. In his message of that year he mentioned the boundary dispute with England, and expressed a hope for the restoration of diplomatic intercourse between that Republic and Great Britain, and for the reference of this question to arbitration.*

Other questions occupied the public mind, and the Venezuelan controversy was allowed to slumber until the autumn of 1895, when persistent rumours appeared in the American press to the effect that the Government of the United States had intervened on behalf of Venezuela. There were numerous statements as to the nature of this interference, and in September the New York *Tribune* professed to have information that the English Government had expressed disapproval of the attitude adopted by America; whilst the Cabinet at Washington was represented as awaiting with great impatience a categorical reply to a despatch from the Secretary of State. These telegrams did not engage particular notice on this side of the Atlantic. There was no satisfactory evidence

* Message to 53rd Congress, 2nd Session, 1893.

where the reports originated, and they were only inter-preted as suggesting the probability that the dimly remembered controversy was likely to be revived before long.

When Congress opened on December 2nd, 1895, the President said:

"The boundary of British Guiana still remains in dispute between Great Britain and Venezuela. Believing that its early settlement, on some just basis alike honour-able to both parties, is in the line of our established policy to remove from this hemisphere all causes of difference with Powers beyond the sea, I shall renew the efforts heretofore made to bring about a restoration of diplomatic relations between the disputants, and to induce a reference to arbitration, a resort which Great Britain so conspicuously favours in principle, and respects in practice, and which is earnestly sought by her weaker adversary."

A few days afterwards it was announced that Lord Salisbury's answer had arrived; and on Tuesday, December 17th, the whole correspondence was sent to both Houses, with a message which at once produced intense excitement throughout the Union.

To properly understand and appreciate this amazing manifesto, it must be read in conjunction with the previous despatch of Mr. Olney, published along with the message. Menacing as was the language of that document, it was calm and dignified in comparison with the gratuitous insolence of the Secretary of State.

Mr. Olney commenced by disclaiming an intention "to enter into any detailed account of the controversy between Great Britain and Venezuela respecting the western frontier of the colony of British Guiana." He then proceeded to argue hypothetically that if the allegations of Venezuela were well founded, this small State was suffering considerable hardship from its more powerful neighbour. In a brief summary of the previous history occur such phrases as "exploitation of the Schomburgk line" by England; "new appropriations of what is claimed to be Venezuelan territory continued to be made"; "new and flagrant British aggressions"; the British claim upon "a shifting footing"; whilst Venezuela is alleged to have made "a liberal concession to her antagonist," "earnest and repeated efforts to have the boundary settled." In 1882 that oppressed community "concluded that the only course open to her was arbitration of the controversy." It was conceded that diplomatic intercourse between England and Venezuela had been terminated by the act of the latter Power, and that the Republic had refused to renew it except on the condition that England should refer the whole dispute to arbitration.

"It is not admitted, however, and, therefore, cannot be assumed, that Great Britain is, in fact, usurping dominion over Venezuelan territory. While Venezuela charges such usurpation, Great Britain denies it, and the United States, until the merits are authoritatively ascertained, can take sides with neither. But while this is so—while the United States may not, under existing circumstances at least, take upon itself to say which of the two parties is right and which wrong—*it is certainly within its right to demand that the truth shall be ascertained.*"

It was not suggested that England was about to assert her claims by force. The mere fact that she continued

looking over the Venezuelan hedge was intolerable, and
notwithstanding the acknowledged uncertainty of the
rights on either side, Mr. Bayard was instructed to press
for a " definite decision " before the meeting of Congress,
" whether Great Britain will consent, or will decline, to
submit the Venezuelan boundary question in its entirety
to impartial arbitration."

By way of explaining the attitude adopted by the
Government of the United States, the larger portion of
the despatch was devoted to the exposition of a famous
declaration made by President Monroe. That statesman's message of 1823 is described as a "part of
American public law "; and in order to lend grace
to the communication, and render it more acceptable
to the Power to which it was addressed, the Secretary
added :

" That distance and 3000 miles of intervening ocean
make any permanent political union between an European
and an American State unnatural and inexpedient, will
hardly be denied. But physical and geographical considerations are the least of the objections to such a union.
Europe, as Washington observed, has a set of primary
interests, which are peculiar to herself. America is not
interested in them, and ought not to be vexed or com-
plicated with them."

There are, at least, four European Powers with
possessions in or adjoining the American continent,
whilst the Power which Mr. Olney was addressing finds
in the American continent the most popular and flourishing of her colonies—a community whose sympathies with
Great Britain, and willingness to share in the trials of the

mother country, have been nobly evinced on more than one occasion. *

If Mr. Olney's proposition of the three thousand miles limit had any bearing on the subject of the despatch, it came to this: England was so habitually in the wrong in her assumption of authority over remote parts of the world, that the probability of her being wrong in the case of Venezuela was increased manifold.

But the Secretary of State was not content with warning Great Britain that the sooner she severed her connection with the American continent the better. He proceeded to point out that there were great moral distinctions between Republics and Monarchies, and to suggest to his Canadian neighbours that they were under a system of government which, from the American point of view, was out of harmony with the sentiment of that continent and fraught with evil results.

" What is true of the material is no less true of what may be termed the moral interests involved. Those pertaining to Europe are peculiar to her, and are entirely diverse from those pertaining and peculiar to America. Europe as a whole is Monarchical: and, with the single important exception of the Republic of France, is committed to the Monarchical principle: America, on the other hand, is devoted to the exactly opposite principle,—to the idea that every people have an inalienable right of self-government. . . . . Whether moral or material interests be considered, it cannot but be universally conceded that those of Europe are irreconcilably diverse

---

* See the brilliant debate in the Dominion House of Commons on Mr. McNeill's motion, 5th February, 1896.

from those of America, and that any European control of the latter is necessarily both incongruous and injurious."

Monarchies are reminded that "the people of the United States have a vital interest in the cause of popular self-government, ... and might not impossibly be wrought up to an active propaganda in favour of a course so highly valued for themselves and for mankind."

Were it possible to conceive a despatch of this character sent by one European Power to another, there can be little doubt that the result would have been the transmission of his passport to the ambassador who presented it. The foreign despatches, however, of an American Secretary of State have only occasionally any international significance. They are generally compiled with a view to home consumption. This paper was read in part by Mr. Bayard to Lord Salisbury on the 7th August, when the new ministers were hardly yet in possession of their offices after the general election of July. Lord Salisbury observed that "the invocation of doctrines so far-reaching in their scope, and containing so much disputable matter, was not calculated to bring to a very early conclusion the controversy respecting the boundary of British Guiana," but he promised to consult the advisers of the Foreign Office as to the facts of the case. On the 26th of November two despatches of the same date were addressed to Mr. Olney. In the second of these Lord Salisbury sketched the history of our controversy with Venezuela, and showed that there was no ground for the allegation of oppression, of which Mr. Olney had assumed the probability. It is, however, with the first despatch that we are at present concerned. In this the English Minister pointed out, that the language of Monroe related to a particular conjuncture of international affairs which had altogether passed away; that however useful at that date, there was nothing in existing circumstances to make it relevant to the Guiana question, or indeed to any other question likely to arise at the present day; that moreover, however venerable, as a guide to American statesmen, the principle laid down might be, it had never become a part of international law, and therefore could not explain the position assumed by the United States on the present occasion; that the principle of arbitration was one to which England was not unfavourable, but it was not applicable to all circumstances, and that each nation must determine in its own discretion when recourse could be had to it.

Mr. Olney's appeal to the name of President Monroe has provoked much comment on both sides of the Atlantic. The history of that President's message of 1823 is admirably told by Lord Salisbury. It is mere trifling to contend that it has any bearing on the dispute between England and Venezuela; England does not seek to appropriate for new settlements any portion of the American continent as if it were a new country, nor is she engaged in any enterprise against the political institutions of any American population. But around the Monroe declaration have clustered a number of popular ideas, which, although they have not been formulated in such clear terms as the President used,

and have even less claims to recognition by foreign
nations, do constitute a distinct part of public opinion
within the Union.

Monroe's original principle may be stated thus : that
without departing from the policy of reserve enjoined
by Washington, the Union ought to resist any attempt
by European nations to coerce American communities
in their choice of a form of government. In the popular
imagination, however, this message fills a much larger
space. It is the germ of a positive foreign policy as
distinguished from the negations of Washington and
Jefferson—a policy confined, it is true, to the American
continent. It is frequently alluded to without any examination of its exact terms, and has been assumed
to claim a sort of primacy for the Union over the
American Republics. As the Union grew stronger and
increased its territories, this idea was expanded into
the theory that the Union ought to have a voice in
any dispute between American States and European
Governments. These notions had never been formulated,
even by American statesmen, and had no possible claim
to recognition by, or authority with, foreign nations ;
but they filled the thoughts of the people within the
Union, and were frequently referred to as part of the
Monroe principle. They are examples of those special
views of foreign policy of which every foreign office has
a selection peculiar to itself. There are certain aims of
policy which a foreign department, properly organized,
keeps in mind—purposes of its own country to be
promoted, of foreign countries to be discouraged—
but they are no portion of international law, and their

direct assertion is only attempted in special circumstances.

As a matter of fact, many American statesmen have
expressly repudiated any assumption of authority which
would involve responsibility for the proceedings of the
Spanish Republics. If, however, it fell in with the policy
of the Cleveland Cabinet to give a new significance to the
communications that pass between the Union and the
South American Governments, it would have been quite
feasible to announce such a development, and leave
foreign countries to determine whether they would
acquiesce in it, or would resist it. Such was the course,
for instance, adopted by Russia in 1876, when she
announced that she would no longer be bound by
the Black Sea clauses of the Treaty of Paris.
The effrontery of the Olney despatch was made conspicuous by the contemptuous indifference to historical
precedent.

In ordinary course the next step, on receipt of the
British reply, would have been for the United States
to have proceeded to justify their interpretation of the
Monroe doctrine, or to show, on other grounds, that
recourse to arbitration might be fittingly pressed upon
Great Britain.

Instead, however, of making any further communication to England, the President, a few days after the
English answer arrived, addressed himself to Congress.
The message bluntly reasserted Mr. Olney's view of the
Monroe principle, but no attempt was made to argue
the matter. The President went on to declare it "incumbent upon the United States to take measures to

determine, with sufficient certainty for its justification, what is the true divisional line between the Republic of Venezuela and British Guiana "; and he requested the Congress to make " an adequate appropriation for the expenses of a Commission to be appointed by the Executive, who shall make the necessary investigations, and report upon the matter with the least possible delay. When such a report is made and accepted, it will, in my opinion, be the duty of the United States to resist, by every means in its power, as a wilful aggression upon its rights and interests, the appropriation by Great Britain of any lands, or the exercise of governmental jurisdiction over any territory *which, after investigation, we have determined of right belong to Venezuela.*

" In making these recommendations, I am fully alive to the responsibility incurred, and keenly realize all the consequences which may follow.

" I am nevertheless firm in my conviction that, while it is a grievous thing to contemplate the two great English-speaking peoples of the world as being otherwise than friendly competitors in the onward march of civilization, and strenuous and worthy rivals in all the arts of peace, there is no calamity which a great nation can invite which equals that which follows a supine submission to wrong and injustice, and the consequent loss of national self-respect and honour, beneath which is shielded and defended a people's safety and greatness."

The message was not read in the Lower House until some time after its tenour had become generally known from the communication to the Senate. It was received by the Republican majority in a crowded sitting with rapturous applause. The Republican party took the lead in the chorus of approval. Major McKinley, of Ohio, the candidate for the Presidency, telegraphed in reference to the message : " It is American in letter and spirit; and, in a calm and dispassionate manner, upholds the honour of the nation, and ensures its security." The New York *Sun*, a Democratic opponent of Mr. Cleveland, said :

"If the eccentric statesman and instinctive antagonist of the more vital American sentiments who now occupies the White House had dealt with the Venezuelan affairs from the beginning in the creditable spirit shown in his message of yesterday, it is a question whether the situation would not now be satisfactory, and without danger of war."

Both Chambers on Wednesday accepted motions made by Republicans—Senator Chandler in the Senate, and Mr. Hitt in the House—to appropriate $100,000 for the expenses of the proposed Commission ; and President Cleveland's popularity rose to such a height that for the next couple of days party distinctions seemed to be effaced. Meanwhile there was a fall in the value of American securities estimated at $400,000,000. For some time previously, apprehensions had been entertained as to the gold reserve. On Friday it had sunk to $72,000,000, whilst both Chambers were preparing to adjourn for the Christmas holidays. Then at five o'clock that day came another message. In it the President referred to his gloomy prognostications at the opening of the Session, and declared that the withdrawal of gold necessitated further provision for protection of the reserve.

" We are in the midst of another season of perplexity, caused by our dangerous and fatuous financial operations.

These may be expected to recur with certainty as long as there is no amendment of our financial system. If in this particular instance our predicament is at all influenced by a recent insistence on the position we should occupy in our relation to certain questions concerning our foreign policy, this furnishes a signal and impressive warning that even the patriotic sentiment of our people is not an adequate substitute for a sound financial policy." *

He asked Congress not to adjourn without lending its aid to "prevent in a time of fear and apprehension any sacrifice of the people's interests and the public funds."

It was promptly announced that the Republicans were willing to assist the President by increasing the import duties. In other words, they proposed to take advantage of the excitement which he had created in order to force him to undo whatever he had achieved in the way of tariff reform. The truce of party struggles which had been made, in view of the ravages of the British Lion, quickly faded away, and Mr. Cleveland resumed the negotiations he had been carrying on for the issue of another loan.

Of this incident numerous explanations have been offered: probably, as in most cases of the kind, the principal actors in it were impelled by a great variety of motives.

One cardinal fact there is of which Englishmen, with their habitual self-complacency, are usually quite unconscious, namely, the strong ingrained prejudice entertained against them by the American people. Anyone who

* *New York Times*, December 21st, 1895.

has more than a superficial acquaintance with the
American continent, is aware that the opinion of the
courteous American who makes so many visits to the
great cities of Europe is not really representative of
the sentiments pervading the masses whose votes decide
elections.   To these latter, with their industry, their
mental activity and limited imagination, England is the
one foreign nation with whom they have some acquaintance.

Their knowledge of history is limited to the annals of
the Union, and these record only two great foreign wars,
both of them with England.   In both, they are taught to
believe, England endeavoured to wrong and oppress them.
Their national independence is the proof of their success
in the first, and in the second they claim some brilliant
achievements.   Whenever they allow themselves time for
anything beyond the making of money, they reflect with
pride on their political institutions; and, in the mouths of
the teachers they listen to, democracy means much more
than a particular form of government.   It is really a creed,
and it absorbs all their enthusiasm.   A belief in
Republican ideas that have given them opportunities of
wealth and power is ever present to them in a concrete
and practical aspect.   If they have any doubt about their
superiority over old countries, they reckon up the thousands
of square miles they have won from the red man and the
bison, traversed by telegraph and railroad, already studded,
most of it, with prosperous cities.   If they have any doubt
of the wickedness of these Old World governments, they
repeat to each other the tales of their childhood about
the tyranny of George III.

The very interesting correspondence to which the
London *Times* opened its columns after the Venezuela
message, reminded the British public of many things we
are too apt to forget. In the first place the proportion
of Americans of English descent is much smaller than
we commonly suppose: Germans and Scandinavians
and the Central European races have contributed largely
to the population of the Mississippi Valley and the
North-west. Their pride, which has its root deep down
in their memory of successful combat with England,
which is fostered by their marvellous material achievements, is mingled with an active element of contempt.
Monarchies seem to them part of the dead past which
their popular poet would efface, and they know that over
the one Monarchy with which they have had practical
relations, they have for sixty years won a long series of
triumphs.

Anglo-American diplomacy has contributed much since
1840 to build up the popular theory of "manifest
destiny." For fifty years after the accession to power
of the English middle classes, the attitude of our country
towards America has been halting and timorous. The
light in which English politicians of that generation
regarded Canada, was disclosed in the writings of the
man who, from his accomplishments and official position,
had a powerful influence over a succession of Colonial
Ministers.* To the minds of Sir Henry Taylor and Lord
Blachford, it was a misfortune that we had found any
shelter for the American loyalists on the banks of the

* *Autobiography of Sir Henry Taylor*, 1888, vol. ii. p. 234.

St. Lawrence, so conscious were they of the aggressive disposition of the United States, and of the disinclination of England to resist.

In accordance with these views, in 1842 we gave up 11,000 square miles of Canadian territory to placate American susceptibility. The boundary of the State of Maine, under the Treaty of 1783, had long been a subject of controversy. Principles of surveying, recognized by President Jackson, pointed to the highlands along the head waters of the Penobscot as those referred to in the treaty—a line nearly 100 miles south of the present frontier. When the Canadians proceeded to construct a railway from New Brunswick to Quebec across this district, Americans invaded it, and after protracted negotiations, Lord Ashburton consented to find the boundary on the north-west branch of the river St. John, and to renounce the watershed of that river. This concession was not merely the abandonment of so much land. The territory relinquished was · essential to the communications of the Dominion, and to the security of the southern frontier.*

Some years before, American pioneers, prospecting beyond the Rocky Mountains, had been chagrined to find that there were British claims over a portion of the region known, then, as Oregon. There was great indignation that the wicked Englishman should venture to show his face on the Pacific, and the watchword of American orators at the Presidential election of 1844 became "Fifty-four forty or fight." These figures indicated

---

* SANDFORD FLEMING's *Intercolonial Railway*. Montreal, 1876.

the parallel of latitude which formed the southern limit of the Russian claims in Alaska, and the phrase meant that the Union and Russia were to have the whole of the Pacific coast to themselves. The British subject was to be driven back, according to this theory, beyond the line of the Rocky Mountains. But the title of England to a substantial share of Oregon could not be denied. It was established, as regards the coast, by a whole series of British discoveries from Drake to Vancouver, and, in the upper waters of the rivers, by Canadian occupation. The only question was the reasonable boundary between British territory and the land acquired by the States from Spain and Mexico northwards. The geographical formation of the country, the interests of Canada, and equity in apportionment of the best lands between the two Powers concerned, were all considerations which pointed to the Columbia River as the proper boundary. This was proposed by England in 1824, but the American Government postponed any settlement. After the first Mexican war the movement to exclude England altogether from the Pacific gained great strength, and on this side of the Atlantic party organs expressed doubts whether Englishmen had any substantial interests on that side of the American continent.* The resources of the Canadian Province of Columbia, north of the Fraser, are enormous, but they were not of obvious and immediate advantage, as were the rich lands, of temperate climate, on either bank of the Columbia River; and this more attractive

---

* *Edinburgh Review,* July, 1845, p. 265.

territory ought, on every principle of equity, to have
been divided between the States which claimed joint
ownership of the vast region between the Mexican and
the Russian frontiers.

By the treaty of 1846, England consented to retire
to the north of the Fraser, thus surrendering some
70,000 square miles of a fertile country, which now
constitutes the State of Washington. Even in accepting
the Fraser as the boundary, no sufficient care was
taken to secure the rights of navigation at the mouth
of the river, and, after long negotiations and a
reference to arbitration, the Island of San Juan was
given up to the States, although it had long been settled
by British subjects.

We may be told that on all such questions compromises
are wiser than contests, and that in coming to an agreement by mutual concession we have won the confidence
of our American neighbours. Mr. Roosevelt may be
taken as a fair example of the class of Americans
who might do justice to such a policy. He is not an
electioneering orator. He is a man of letters, not a
professional politician. Addressing the literary classes
of his countrymen as late as 1889, he says of Benton
and the part that statesman took in the Oregon controversy :

"The arrogant attitude he assumed was more than
justified by the destiny of the great Republic, and it
would have been well for all America if we had insisted
even more than we did upon the extension northward
of our boundaries. Not only the Columbia, but also the
Red River of the North, and the Saskatchewan and

Fraser as well, should lie wholly within our limits—less for our own sake than for the sake of the men who dwell along their banks. Columbia, Saskatchewan and Manitoba would, as States of the American Union, hold positions incomparably more important, grander, and more dignified than they can ever hope to reach either as independent communities or as provincial dependencies of a foreign Power." *

Of this Oregon territory he says, "We are the people who could use it best, and we ought to have taken it all."

The spirit in which the genuine American regards the land of his neighbours is shown still more clearly in the Sherman Letters. It is constantly said that the light-hearted way in which the boundaries between one country and another are alluded to by American statesmen is only harmless bravado for the amusement of the crowd. But in September, 1887, we find† Senator Sherman writing, in the privacy of fraternal intercourse, to consult the General upon the question of appropriating the wide territories to the south and north of the Union.

"If the population of Mexico and Canada," says the Senator, "were homogeneous with ours, the union of the three countries would make the whole the most powerful nation in the world. I am not so sure that this would be a good thing to do." This latter sentence we see, from the General's reply, does not imply any scruples as to a repetition of the devices which led up to the

---

* Roosevelt's *Life of Benton*, p. 266.
† *The Sherman Letters*, by P. Thorndike. Lond. 1894.

Mexican wars. The question is whether aggression would really be useful to the Union. The General says, " My judgment at present is that we want no more territory. If we could take in the territory of Ontario, it would make a good State; but the vast hyperborean region of the North would embarrass us with inchoate States and territories without a corresponding revenue. I am dead against any more of Mexico." Here we have two men of great experience and responsibility, both of whom played memorable parts in the history of their country. They are not addressing noisy crowds, but, in the seclusion of their libraries, they are speculating on the balance of advantage in appropriating the lands of other nations.

Since Benton's time, a great change has come over all these frontier questions, as a result of the constitution of the Dominion; but this growth of a great industrial population, who are not believers in the blessings of Republican government, does not by any means soothe the susceptibilities of the American citizen, whilst his opinion of the nation whom he has defeated, both in the field and in the council chamber, steadily declines. We are constantly told that the Americans are an industrial, not a military, sanguinary race, and this is probably true: but they are eminently manly, and regard with disdain all who affect a position which they do not defend.

One of the popular explanations of the Venezuela message was, that the President's advisers had been alarmed and chagrined by the attacks made on the Government in connection with many parts of his foreign

Q

policy, such as his declarations about Hawaii and Samoa, and his acquiescence in the measures taken by England against Nicaragua earlier in the year 1895. Mr. Olney's despatch was, it is said, intended to restore the credit of the party before the elections in the following November. The urgency of other affairs rendered it impossible for the English Cabinet to deal with this onslaught at the moment, and whilst Mr. Olney's eloquence lay buried in despatch boxes at Whitehall, the State elections came on. The Democratic polls tumbled down by hundreds of thousands. It was not the number of the seats lost, so much as the places where these defeats occurred, which made these elections ominous of the break up of the Democratic majority. New York, Ohio, and Kentucky, States which supported Mr. Cleveland in 1892, were carried by large Republican majorities.

The Cabinet had been deprived of the opportunity of setting themselves right in the opinion of their countrymen, and showing their spirit in dealing with monarchies, and Mr. Cleveland, it is supposed, wrote the Venezuela message under a sense of extreme irritation. This is a somewhat frivolous line of speculation, and proceeds on assumptions for which there does not appear to be any trustworthy foundation. It is supposed that a man of Mr. Cleveland's calibre must be above the passions and prejudices of his nation. Overweening self-complacency makes Englishmen forget how intense and universal these feelings are. The antipathy to monarchies, the jealousy of European connection, have always characterized the most illustrious leaders of that party whose political training he has endeavoured to advance.

They were conspicuous in Benton, Calhoun, and Jackson —men whose teaching every Democrat regards with enthusiasm. It is probable that, although Mr. Cleveland would express himself in a different way, he sympathizes with the republican righteousness of the Morgans, the Dolphs, the Chandlers, and the Lodges, and would be well pleased to have done his part in loosening the ties which connect European Governments with populations on the American continent.

Whether the condition of opinion shown in the speeches and writings of American statesmen, and apparently, to some extent, shared by so able a man as the President, qualifies that country to help in the elaboration of a new system of international relations, it is not necessary here to enquire. The reader's concern is with the acts and motives of Mr. Cleveland; and in estimating the effect of his Venezuelan policy on his claims to statesmanship there is this further consideration, in addition to the mental attitude of Americans towards England, and their disbelief in her willingness to fight. There is the probability that, engrossed in profound questions of home policy, he has not observed the remarkable change which England has undergone since the days of the Ashburton and the Oregon Treaties. One indirect and unexpected result of Mr. Cobden's achievements has been to excite an interest in foreign affairs among numerous classes of Englishmen, who formerly regarded such questions with absolute indifference. The conviction has spread over the country that the foreign policy pursued from Peel to Granville was dangerous and costly, and that we are likely to suffer in our self-respect, our sense of personal security, and in our pockets, until we have succeeded in convincing some nation of the first class that in equipment and resolution we are ready for war.

CHAPTER XV.

THE CHICAGO REVOLT.

Continued exports of gold—Loan of one hundred millions—Loan
Prohibition Bill—River and Harbour Bill—Passed over the
veto—Free coinage agitation—Civil Service reform—Republicans
nominate McKinley—Cleveland calls his party to action—The
Chicago platform—Nomination of Bryan by Democrats at Chicago
and Populists at St. Louis—The Populist party.

IT would not be necessary to devote any further space
to the fifty-fourth Congress, were it not for the
striking contrast which the last session presents in the
exploits of the majority on the one hand, and the un-
shaken spirit of the President on the other. The conflict
between the advocates of free coinage in the Senate, and
the champions of high duties in the House of Representatives, occupied Congress, but brought no help to the
Treasury. The export of gold continued, and in January
preparations were made for the issue of a new loan.

A notice was published, inviting applications for $50
bonds to the amount of $100,000,000 before the 6th
February. The bonds were to bear 4 per cent. interest,
to be paid for in gold, and be repayable in "coin" in
1926. European bankers refused to apply, and the very
day the Treasury proposal was published, the Finance
Committee of the Senate passed the Free Coinage Bill.
Notwithstanding this discouragement, bids came in to the
amount of $558,000,000, some applicants offering as

much as $60 for the $50 bond. The Treasury thus
obtained $111,000,000 in gold. For the next thirty years
a permanent addition of $4,000,000 has been made to the
annual debt charge, because the owners of silver continue
to force their commodity upon Congress.

The more satisfactory arrangement of 1896 has been
used as an argument against the loan of 1895, when a
contract was made with a company of bankers to supply
gold in exchange for bonds; but in the first place the
emergency in 1895 was much more sudden.* In the
second, the country in 1896 had made further experience
of Mr. Cleveland's policy, and relied on his determination to maintain a gold standard.

Long and vehement debates were devoted to Cuba. But
the most notable proceedings of this Congress occurred
towards the close of the session, when the silver agitation
had become formidable throughout the country. Mr.
Butler, the Populist Senator for North Carolina, had
early in the session introduced a bill forbidding the
President to make any more loans under the act of 1875
without the consent of Congress. Suddenly a prominent
place was given to this measure, of which the avowed
purpose was to prevent payment in gold and compel the
Treasury to pay in silver. When the bill was brought on
for debate (May 21st) only five Democrats recorded their
votes against it, and it was carried in the Senate; but the
House of Representatives rejected it by a large majority.
These divisions marked the lines of the Presidential contest. After the prompt rejection of Mr. Butler's bill by the

* Mr. Carlisle's evidence before Bond Committee of the Senate,
June 9, 1896.

House, it gradually became evident that the Republicans had made up their minds to resist the proposal of free coinage.

About the same time there was sent to the President for approval a River and Harbour Bill, over which Congress had been busy for some months. The prolonged discussion upon it did not arise from any disposition to protect the Treasury. The difficulty was the number of applicants for a share in the spoil. The opposition to expenditure of this kind out of the Federal taxes was a cherished principle of the Democrats as long ago as the Presidency of Madison; and now, at a time of general depression, miscellaneous demands were made on the taxpayer to the amount of $80,000,000. "There are 417 items in this bill," said the President in his veto message, "and every part of the country is represented in the distribution of its favours." He added:

"Many of the objects for which it appropriates public money are not related to the public welfare, and many of them are palpably for the benefit of limited localities, or in aid of individual interests. . . . .

"I believe no greater danger confronts us as a nation than the unhappy decadence among our people of genuine and trustworthy love and affection for our Government as the embodiment of the highest and best aspirations of humanity, and not as the giver of gifts, and because its mission is the enforcement of exact justice and equality, and not the allowance of unfair favouritism."

The project was the more reckless at a time when there was a deficit of forty millions. The protest of Mr. Cleveland will be remembered hereafter, but it could have no restraining influence upon politicians whose sole aim was to recommend themselves to their constituents before the November election. The Constitution

gave them the power to override the veto by a two-
thirds majority.   This was readily secured in both
Houses, and the bill became law.

Early in May, Mr. Cleveland issued an order adding
30,000 more posts in the Civil Service to the list of those
for which a certificate of competence from the Civil
Service Commissioners is a necessary qualification.
When he became President in 1885, there were only
some 13,000 public appointments, out of 130,000, for
which any test of this kind was requisite.   Ever since
the first term of Jackson in 1829, a change of parties
had been followed invariably by the removal of all
subordinate officials, the supporters of the new President
being, as a matter of course, installed in every department.   The example set by Jackson had been approved
by Taylor, and followed by Lincoln.   Nearly the whole
public service had been changed when Lincoln assumed
office in 1861.   Coming into power at the head of a
party who for a whole generation had been excluded
from public employment, Mr. Cleveland refused to follow
the precedent set by Jackson.   Before he left office, he
added 20,000 to the number of posts to which the Civil
Service Act was applicable.   When he returned to power,
he again refused to act on the "spoils system," although
in 1889 President Harrison had applied it with the utmost
rigour ; and this year he has raised the number of
appointments for which certificates from the Civil Service
Commission are required to over 80,000.*

He thus practically broke up the "spoils system" for
ever, unless indeed Mr. W. J. Bryan and his friends

* *New York Times*, May 7th, 1896.

succeed in repealing the Pendleton Act. The firmness with which the President has carried out this policy is the more deserving of notice from the violence with which he has been attacked by Civil Service reformers on the one hand, and by Democratic place-hunters on the other. The history of the Civil Service in America throws a very interesting light on the working of Democratic institutions, did space permit of its examination. In no other branch of administration have Mr. Cleveland's resolute pursuit of the public good, and indifference to popular clamour, been more conspicuous.

In Congress, however, and outside Congress, the great question of the year was the preparation for the twenty-eighth Presidential election.

The victories of the Republicans at two successive polls made it highly probable that they would secure the control of administration in 1896, and the public were much interested in the choice that party might make of a candidate. Mr. L. P. Morton, the Republican Governor of New York, frankly announced his willingness to stand. In finance he was a supporter of the Cleveland policy, but on tariff questions he went with his party. He had already held the office of Vice-President during the Harrison term, and his repute as an upright, able man gave him considerable weight as a candidate. The only objection to him, in the eyes of independent Republicans, was, that he had the support of the party machine; and his success, they argued, would mean the supremacy of these politicians in New York State. Next in importance was the Speaker, Mr. Reed, who, as the fighting man of the party, enjoyed a widespread popularity.

Before the year had been many months old, it became
evident that the hero of the 1890 tariff was the favourite
candidate of the Western States. His success in 1890
had been followed by swift ruin; his party was swept
away for the time, and his law repealed with ignominy;
and now, six years afterwards, the masses of his countrymen were returning to his standard. His position on
the tariff was pretty well understood. He might not be
quite so McKinleyite in 1896 as in 1890; but he was
in favour of high duties on all foreign goods, and the
reservation of the American market for American
producers. On the subject of currency, his views were not
so well known. He had voted for the silver men, and
had denounced their opponents. Mr. Cleveland he had
held up to reproach for having "struck down silver";
but this was not a subject on which he was directly
pledged, as on tariff, and he was immediately challenged
to say whether he was for free coinage or for the gold
standard. It is characteristic of Republican politics that
this demand was denounced with indignation. It was
a barefaced attempt to hamper an "available" candidate.
He was actually asked to come out and say what he
thought about a subject which, as events showed, moved
the country more deeply than any other. These extravagant questioners expected him to risk losing thousands of
votes in order to gratify their misplaced curiosity.

One of his sponsors, General Grosvenor, said:

"No man's friends have a right to call upon him to
foreshadow the party's platform. . . . Major McKinley
will *respond to the platform*, but he will not dictate what
the platform shall be." *

* *New York Times*, May 18th, 1896.

Meantime the Eastern States declared in clear terms for a gold standard; and their delegates soon made it evident that whilst they might exercise their discretion in the choice of a candidate, they were pledged against a change in the standard of money.

There was ominous delay in the settlement of the declaration of policy; but at length, on the 18th June, it was reported with a paragraph against the free coinage of silver.*

The Democrats and their administration were vehemently denounced. For the first time since the Civil War that party had possessed full and unrestricted control of the Government, and the decline in revenue, the adverse balance of trade, the addition of $262,000,000 to the debt, were all cited as so many proofs of incapacity and mismanagement, in contrast with the wisdom and patriotism of the Harrison Cabinet. As regards import duties, the Republicans demanded such a rate of duty on the foreign imports which came into competition with American products as would not only furnish adequate revenue for the necessary expenses of the Government, but would " protect American labour from degradation to

---

* "We are unalterably opposed to every measure calculated to debase our currency, or impair the credit of our country. We are, therefore, opposed to the free coinage of silver, *except by international agreement with the leading commercial nations of the world, which we pledge ourselves to promote ;* and *until such agreement can be obtained*, the existing gold standard must be preserved. All our silver and paper currency must be maintained at parity with gold; and we favour all measures designed to maintain inviolably the obligations of the United States, and all our money, whether coin or paper, at the present standard, the standard of the most enlightened nations of the earth."

the wage level of other lands." " Protection," it is added, " builds up domestic industry and trade, and secures our own markets for ourselves."

On the adoption of this platform, it became evident that the controversy between the Western and the Eastern Republicans had been compromised at the expense of the Eastern candidates, and Major McKinley secured the nomination. The party were opposed to the free coinage demand, although no further light was thrown on their financial policy, whether they would return to the Sherman Act as well as the McKinley Act, or how they might in the future deal with the champions of silver. They were in favour of the gold standard; but so was President Harrison when he signed the Sherman Act. In a few days Mr. McKinley declared his complete adherence to the platform; but he said nothing to make it more definite, and continued to urge the necessity of tariff legislation.*

The Democrats summoned their Convention for the 7th July, and it was noticed with surprise that no Democratic candidates had been put distinctly before the public. Mr. Carlisle and Mr. Whitney were both named, and many influential journals urged that Mr. Cleveland ought to stand again, although there is a tradition that election for a third term is too great an honour to bestow on anyone in the land of universal equality.

Before May was over, it had become clear that the Democratic organizers throughout the West, and a large part of the South, had enlisted under the silver banner. The party leaders, not expecting to carry the election, gave themselves very little trouble, and the professional

* Speech to the Knoxville Deputation, July 30th.

politicians, left to follow their own inclinations, were
tempted by the local outcry for more currency, and by
their animosity to Mr. Cleveland. Twelve years ago he
had been put over their heads, because he was not one
of them. For eight years of that time he had, as he
himself expresses it, been "engaged in a hand-to-hand
fight with the bad elements of both parties."* He had
held up their schemes and their methods to public repro-
bation, and destroyed that system of patronage on which
they depended for their own subsistence and that of their
friends. He had pursued this course from some Quixotic
theory of duty towards the man in the street, towards
the labourer in the fields ; and now his ungrateful clients,
smarting under the pricks of poverty, were clamouring for
the undoing of everything which he had achieved ; whilst
the activity and resources of the Bimetallic Associations
had rallied all this discontent to the support of the free
coinage movement. Here was an opportunity at least for
vengeance, perhaps for a new career of peculation. Some
weeks before the Convention met, it was evident that
the Free Silver party would have an absolute majority,
possibly a majority of two-thirds. The only question was,
what fight the advocates of a gold standard would make.

When the apostasy to silver became known to all the
world, the leaders were still hesitating, and seemed
inclined to postpone any trial of strength until 1900.
Then, on the 16th June, Mr. Cleveland, as head of
the party, published a stirring manifesto. The free silver
movement, he declared, was too extravagant to survive
discussion. "It must be that many of the illusions

influencing those now relying on this alleged panacea for
their ills, will be dispelled before the time comes for them
to cast their ballots." He went on to set out the true
theory of a National Convention. It was not a mere
registering machine, but an opportunity for conference
and consultation. If such a mistake as the adoption of
free coinage was likely to be made, it was the duty of
every sensible member of the party to take his share in
the work, and do what he could to guard against the
mischief. "A cause worth fighting for," he added, "is
worth fighting for to the end." This letter aroused his
followers to activity. Many well-known men, who had
determined to keep away from Chicago, announced their
intention to take part in the Convention.

The temper of that assembly was soon manifest. The
reports of the National Committee were promptly set
aside. A Southern supporter of silver, Senator Daniel,
was put in the chair in place of the chairman named
by the Committee, the Michigan delegates were unseated,
and a two-thirds majority secured. Then came the
declaration of policy, which was in effect an indictment
of President Cleveland, although neither he nor the
Cabinet were expressly mentioned. The Committee on
Resolutions blamed whatever he had done or recom-
mended, and praised whatever he had condemned.
There had been rumours that he would be again nominated, and accordingly they declared it to be the
unwritten law of the Republic that "no man should be
eligible for a third term of the Presidential office."

To make their animus still more clear, meeting in the
city which had been the scene of President Cleveland's

intervention against the Debs movement in 1894, they introduced a eulogy on "the dual system of government," and added that the National Government ought to be confined to the "exercise of powers granted by the Constitution of the United States." In a subsequent paragraph they said, "We denounce arbitrary interference by Federal authorities in local affairs as a violation of the Constitution, and a crime against free institutions." On currency, on the increase of the powers of the Executive, on questions of public order, on the policy of the Treasury, on Civil Service reform, on Cuba, they were opposed to the President. Even in regard to tariff they took pains to differ. Tariff duties, they said, should be levied for purposes of revenue ; but the word " only" was left out, and thus the principle to which Mr. Cleveland had recalled the party in 1887 was obscured. They added that they were opposed to any changes in tariff until the money question was settled. The decision of the Supreme Court against the legality of the income tax was denounced in strong terms.

After this startling manifesto, it was still uncertain who would receive the nomination. The speech of Mr. Bryan, of Nebraska, in defence of the platform, had excited the wildest enthusiasm, and next day he was nominated by a large majority. The delegates from the Eastern States, after a stout fight in the committees, retained their seats as observers, but refused to take any further part in the proceedings. The primary motive of the organizers was evidently to get rid of Mr. Cleveland. Who succeeded him was a matter of secondary consideration.

The Populist Convention met at St. Louis, and, after some discussion, determined not to run a candidate of their own, but to adopt Mr. Bryan, and their leaders have since been busy on his behalf.

This new party includes the remnants of a number of factions which have maintained irrational theories on currency and finance during the last twelve years, but they have hitherto been recruited chiefly at the expense of the Republicans in the North-West. Mr. Weaver was their leader in 1880, when they demanded the continuance of the greenback currency. In 1892 they made a formidable show as supporters of free coinage, winning some seats in the South at the expense of the Democrats, and polling 1,122,000 votes for the Presidency. Their support of Mr. Bryan is not likely to improve his chances in the Southern States, and the movement which was started after Mr. Cleveland's manifesto in favour of asserting the principles of the Democrats, has made rapid progress. A new Convention of the party has been called for the 2nd September. Meanwhile, Senator Gorman, of Maryland, and the Tammany following in New York City are pledged to Mr. Bryan. An admirable opportunity is thus provided for testing the vitality of Democratic principles apart from those elements which have hitherto discredited the party among patriotic Americans. Whatever be the result, Mr. Cleveland's attempt to apply the original teaching of Jefferson and his followers to the Republic of to-day will remain the most interesting chapter in American History since the Civil War.

W. Brendon and Son, Printers, Plymouth.